# Christmas Stories

## A collection of festive tales

# Christmas Stories

Chosen by Lauren Buckland

Illustrated by Hannah George

MACMILLAN CHILDREN'S BOOKS

First published 2006 by Macmillan Children's Books

This edition published 2015 by Macmillan Children's Books
an imprint of Pan Macmillan
20 New Wharf Road, London N1 9RR
Associated companies throughout the world
www.panmacmillan.com

ISBN 978-1-4472-8493-2

1 3 5 7 9 8 6 4 2

A CIP catalogue record for this book is available from the British Library.

Typeset by Nigel Hazle
Printed and bound by CPI Group (UK) Ltd, Croydon CR0 4YY

*For Mum and Helen —Merry Christmas!*

# Contents

# The Pirates' Christmas Party

## Adèle Geras

'**A**fter you've both finished your pudding,' said Beth, 'you can listen to what I wrote at school today. It was so good that Mrs Barnes made me read it out in front of the whole class.'

'What have we done to deserve it?' said Andy, Beth's brother, and their mother said: 'Be quiet, Andy. We listen to you often enough, going on and on about this and that.'

She smiled at Beth. 'We'd love to hear it.'

'What's it about?' said Andy, sighing. 'Go on, get it over with.'

'It's called "My Best Christmas Present Ever". Are you ready? I'll stand up so that you can hear me properly.'

'We're all together round the table,' said Mum. 'We're not in the Albert Hall. I think you can stay sitting down.'

'I'll go and get it out of my school bag then,' said Beth. 'Don't anybody move.'

She was back almost at once, holding a big sheet of paper. Andy groaned.

'It's not long, is it?' he said. 'Some of us have got stuff to do.'

'It's as long as it has to be,' said Beth, 'to say what I want it to say.'

'Get on with it then,' said Andy.

'Right,' said Beth. 'I will.' She coughed and sat up very straight in her chair:

'"My Best Christmas Present Ever, by Beth Johnston. Class 4.

'"My dad works on an oil rig, and last year he had to stay on the rig over Christmas. He sent me a present from Scotland. It is a ship in a bottle. The ship is called a galleon. My dad says that ships are always called 'she', like girls. She has three masts and lovely white sails, and a figurehead of a red fish with blue eyes. She is very beautiful. My brother Andrew is ten years old, and he likes pirates. He said she was a pirate ship. Dad said I could call her anything I wanted, so I decided

on the *Crimson Cod*. I put the bottle with the ship in it on the table next to my bed, and when I go to sleep, I wish I could get very tiny and wake up on board the galleon, as a cabin girl."

'There.' Beth beamed at her mother and brother. 'What did you think of that?'

'Not bad,' said Andy, 'and quite short, really.'

'It was lovely!' said Mum. 'Keep it to show Dad when he gets back tomorrow. Now, who's going to help me with the dishes?'

The last thing Beth did before she got into bed was open a door on her Advent calendar. December 14. Tomorrow was the last day of school. There would be turkey and roast potatoes in the canteen, and everyone singing carols in the afternoon. Then came the ten days before Christmas: the best ten days of the year. Beth loved choosing gifts and making decorations and finding exactly the right tree,

and writing Christmas cards and wrapping all the presents in special paper covered with pictures of Santa and his reindeer. She longed to make a snowman, and wished they lived in a colder part of the country.

Beth spent a lot of time wishing and when she wasn't wishing, she was imagining. Sometimes she pretended she was a princess, and sometimes that she was one of King Arthur's knights. Sometimes she imagined that she lived in the dolls' house under the window, and was friends with her dolls, but the very best games of all were the ones she played with Andy. He didn't play with her as often as she would have liked, but the Pirate Game was Beth's favourite. Andy said that 'Andrew' wasn't a very piratical name, so he became Captain Cutlass Caleb and she was his trusty cabin girl, Buccaneer Beth.

She lay in bed and turned on her side so that she could look at the *Crimson Cod*, safe in her bottle. Someone had painted green and blue waves on the glass, so that it really looked as though the little galleon was flying through the water. Perhaps, thought Beth, they were on their way to search for buried treasure. She closed her eyes. Suddenly, it seemed as though her whole bed was rocking gently to and fro . . .

Beth sat up. She blinked and rubbed her eyes. Where was her bedroom? What had happened to her bed? And why wasn't she wearing her pyjamas with spacemen on them? She seemed to be in a hammock, in a long, low room, dimly lit by one lantern. There were other hammocks, slung from beams in the ceiling, and in them Beth could see . . .

'Pirates!' she cried aloud, and rolled out of her hammock and on to the floor. 'You're all pirates! I'm on a pirate ship. Wake up, please! Help!' She could hear snores all around her.

She peered into the nearest hammock and saw a pink-faced man with a long, ginger beard, sleeping with his mouth

open. She prodded him.

'Avast, me hearties . . .' he mumbled, and opened his eyes. 'Oh, 'tis you, Buccaneer Beth. Pass me the rum, there's a good cabin girl.'

'Who are you?' asked Beth. The ginger beard shook and wobbled while the pirate laughed.

'I'm Ginger George,' he said, 'as well you know, Beth m'dear.'

The other pirates began to wake up. Beth decided to watch and listen and pretend that she knew exactly what was going on. I'm dreaming, she said to herself. I was looking at the *Crimson Cod* before I fell asleep and now I'm dreaming that I'm aboard a pirate ship. I shall wake up soon, so I'm not going to worry.

Breakfast on board a pirate ship turned out to be hard biscuits dipped in cold beer.

'Don't you have cornflakes?' Beth asked Ginger George. 'Or toast and marmalade?'

'Them's for landlubbers,' said Fearsome Four-Eye Fergal, a skinny pirate who wore glasses and didn't seem fearsome at all.

After breakfast, Beth followed the others up on deck.

''Tis time,' said Fergal, 'to swab the decks and mizzen the mainmast and swizzle the sails.' Beth had never heard of swizzling the sails, so she pointed to a small, round man in a red coat. He had an eye patch and a long twirly moustache. Beth said:

'Is that the Captain?'

'You know it is,' Fergal answered. 'That's Black-Hearted Basil, the Scourge of the Seven Seas and Captain of the *Crimson Cod*.'

'Are we sailing on the *Crimson Cod*?' Beth wanted to know.

'You're asking more daft questions than there's weevils in the flour, lass. Surely you know what your own ship is called?'

Beth said nothing. A terrible thought occurred to her. What if she wasn't

8

dreaming? What if there really *was* such a thing as wishes coming true? What if she truly *was* on board a pirate ship? Would she ever get back to her real life? For a moment she felt like crying. I'm never going to make a wish again, she said to herself. And what about Christmas? She said to Fergal: 'Are you going to do anything exciting for Christmas?'

'Never do,' said Fergal. 'Not as long as I've been at sea.'

'No presents?'

'No.'

'No turkey or mince pies?'

'No.'

'Don't you hang out your stockings on Christmas Eve?'

Fergal shook his head.

'What about singing carols?'

'We sing sea shanties,' said Fergal. 'Never heard of no carols.'

'I wish,' said Beth, 'to see the Captain.'

'The Captain's a busy man,' said Fergal.

'I doubt he'll have the time to bandy words with the likes of you.'

Beth, however, was quite determined to speak to Black-Hearted Basil and so Fergal led her to his cabin door. She knocked on it three times.

'Enter!' said a pleasant, rather soft voice.

Beth opened the door, and tried not to stare. Black-Hearted Basil was sitting on a sofa, knitting. Beside him was a gigantic white, fluffy cat who looked just like a round cushion that had had two green eyes sewn on it. All around the cabin were straw baskets overflowing with balls of wool in every colour you could possibly imagine, and there was an embroidery frame in one corner, where Basil had just started work on a tapestry. The picture painted on the canvas was of a country cottage and a garden full of flowers. Beth looked at it in amazement.

'You're admiring my tapestry, I see,' said Basil. 'It's a new hobby of mine. I've only

ever done knitting and crochet before, so I
thought I'd branch out.'

'I never knew,' said Beth, 'that pirates did
things like knitting.'

'Well, the days at sea are endlessly long,
my duck, and there's only so much swabbing
and mizzening and shinning up the rigging
that a chap can do all at once.'

'But what about boarding other ships and

11

stealing their cargo? Burying treasure and making maps of where it's to be found? What about making people walk the plank?' Beth sounded quite plaintive.

'Oh, we do all those things occasionally, of course. When the need arises, you might say. But it does still leave me an awful lot of time to pursue my hobbies. Do you like what I'm making now?' He held up his knitting so that Beth could see it better. 'It's a fiendishly difficult Fair Isle pattern, but this waistcoat will be a thing of beauty, mark my words.'

Beth coughed. If she didn't say something soon, the Captain would keep her there discussing knitting patterns for ages. She said:

'Please, sir, I'd like to organize a Christmas party.'

'Christmas?' The Captain counted off a few stitches and muttered to himself for a moment. 'Is it Christmas already?'

'Yes, sir, and I think we should have a party. We could decorate the ship, and the

Cook could make a cake, and we could sing carols. I don't suppose we could get hold of a Christmas tree, but I'm sure everyone would love a party.'

The Captain sucked the end of a knitting needle and said: 'Decorations . . . decorations . . . that rings a bell . . . I'm sure that somewhere in here . . .' He smiled at Beth. 'Please forgive me. I've been at sea so long that I've forgotten what some of these old chests have actually got in them, only I have a distinct memory of my old mum saying something about Christmas, last time she packed my sea-chests. Let's have a little look.'

Black-Hearted Basil laid his knitting down on the sofa.

'Morgan,' he said to the cat, 'don't you dare chew my wool.' Morgan yawned as though wool-chewing would be altogether too much effort, and closed his eyes for a nap. Black-Hearted Basil began to rummage, first

13

in one chest, then in another.

'Here we are!' he cried at last. 'I knew it! Here's enough decorations for an entire fleet of ships!'

Beth couldn't believe her eyes. There were rolls of tinsel, coloured glass balls, paper lanterns, yards and yards of red ribbon, little bottles full of glitter, a bag full of assorted gold and silver stars, plastic holly and mistletoe, and right at the bottom of the chest, a little Christmas tree, carefully wrapped up in a polythene bag.

'That's my mum all over,' said Basil. 'She thinks of everything. Real Christmas trees shed their needles all over the carpet, but this little imitation one . . . well, it's quite lovely, don't you agree?'

'It's perfect,' said Beth. 'Now we can have a really wonderful Christmas party. I shall go and talk to the Cook at once.'

'And I shall summon the crew on to the deck and address them all. I don't do that

very often and I shall enjoy it. Come and listen, before you go down and talk to Cook.'

Beth and the Captain went up on deck. The First Mate, Desperate Bertie, rang the bell that called the pirates from every corner of the *Crimson Cod*. When they had gathered into a raggedy crowd, Black-Hearted Basil raised his hand for silence.

'Our esteemed cabin girl, Buccaneer Beth, has had a splendid idea. We are going to have a Christmas party!'

The crew cheered loudly, and several of the pirates threw their caps in the air and whistled.

'Now,' the Captain continued, 'has anyone got anything at all Christmassy tucked away in their sea-going bundles? I want you all to have a good look and tell young Beth what you come up with . . . We will all assemble here again in one hour.'

The pirates hurried away to look through their belongings. After an hour, they came up on deck once more, and Beth made a list of everything they had found. The list read:

1 *box of assorted crackers* – Peg-leg Percy
2 *boxes of mixed streamers* – Browntooth Billy
1 *set of angel chimes (with candles)* – One-Arm Eric
3 *sets of paper napkins (holly and bells pattern)* – Jabez the Knife
1 *fairy doll (for top of tree)* – Silent Angus
1 *Santa Claus costume* – Ginger George
1 *mouth organ* – Fearsome Fergal

'That's a very good list,' said Beth. 'Thank you all very much indeed.'

'I'll tell you what I've found,' said Desperate Bertie, 'and that's a bundle of knitted stockings. The Captain tried to interest me in knitting, aargh, a good few years ago now, but I only ever got the hang of stockings. P'raps we can hang 'em on our hammocks, come Christmas Eve, and Ginger George can dress up in that there costume of

his, and fill 'em all with ship's biscuits!'

'What a good idea, Bertie!' said Beth. 'Please go and find them. Each man at the party can have one and that will be their going-home present. You can't have a proper party without a present to take home. We'll get Ginger George to give them out.'

The next few hours were spent in frantic preparations. Cross-Eyed Colin, the Cook of the *Crimson Cod* (who never left his kitchen, even in a Force Ten gale), had been persuaded to open his secret larder, and in it there were enough good things to make:

1    *enormous fruitcake*
24   *mince pies*
2    *gallons of brandy sauce*

The younger members of the crew climbed the rigging and tied coloured tinsel to the tops of the sails. They fixed the biggest gold star of all to the very top of the tallest mast,

where it caught the sun and twinkled brightly enough to dazzle the passing sea birds. Down on the deck, a big spare sail was unrolled and spread out like a tablecloth, and Jabez the Knife (who had once done a three-week course in Flower Arrangement) had decorated the table with sprigs of imitation holly and paper napkins in the shape of roses. There was a cracker beside every plate, and the angel chimes made a pretty centrepiece. The Captain's Christmas tree, with Silent Angus's fairy doll right at the top of it, stood on an upturned bucket, which had been cunningly covered in red crêpe paper to make it look festive. Cross-Eyed Colin ventured up on deck for the first time in years to set out the food, and Beth poured rum into every glass.

When all the pirates had sat down, Beth said:

'The first thing we must do is pull our crackers and put on our paper hats.'

This took some time, while the pirates

giggled and shrieked and swapped hats with
one another, because there were some people
who didn't think blue suited them, and others
who said they'd rather not wear orange,
thank you very much.

Then came the eating and drinking.
Everyone agreed it was the best feast ever
to be spread on the deck of the *Crimson
Cod*. There wasn't a single pirate who didn't
have to loosen his waistband before long,
and Ginger George, magnificent in his Santa
Claus outfit, began muttering about going on
a diet. Beth stood up. She said:

'Thank you all very much for helping to
make this such a lovely party. Before Ginger
George gives you all your knitted stockings
as a present, I'd like you to join in with this
Christmas sea shanty I've made up. It's very
easy to learn.'

'Yes!' shouted the pirates. 'Sing us a
Christmas shanty, lass!'

Beth coughed a little and began to sing:

*'Paper hats and a sprig of holly,*
*A cracker to pull with a yo-ho-ho.*
*Tinsel on the sails looks oh, so jolly.*
*It's Christmas time, so yo-heave-ho.*
*Fill our Christmas stockings with nice surprises,*
*Yo-ho-ho and a bell to ring.*
*Nuts and oranges and fat mince pie-ses.*
*Sing a Christmas shanty, boys!*
*Sing, sing, sing!'*

Fergal took up the tune on his mouth organ, and soon all the pirates were singing loudly enough to shiver the timbers of the *Crimson Cod*.

After the singing, Ginger George went and found his sack, and the pirates lined up for their gift of one knitted stocking each. Beth said to Bertie:

'They're really beautiful, Bertie. You never told me they were stripy.'

'Oh, aye,' said Bertie. 'Not much point to a stocking, unless it's striped. That's what my Auntie Maud always used to say.'

'May I have one as well?' Beth asked.

'Of course,' said Ginger George, plunging his hand into the sack. 'What do you say to stripes of purple and green?'

'Thank you,' said Beth. 'I'll keep it as a souvenir of the party.'

In the end, even the fiercest pirate has to

go to bed. Beth climbed into her hammock, clutching her knitted stocking. The *Crimson Cod* rocked gently on the waves, and Beth fell asleep almost at once.

Suddenly someone was shouting in her ear.

'Come on, lazy Beth!' said her mum's voice. 'School today, you know. You can't lie in until tomorrow.'

Beth opened her eyes and knew at once that she was back in her own bedroom.

'I dreamed I was on a pirate ship last night . . .' she started to say, but Mum was already on her way downstairs.

'Tell me about it later,' she called over her shoulder.

Beth washed and dressed. Then she looked down at the *Crimson Cod*, lying quietly in her glass bottle. Something was glittering at the top of the main mast, and Beth picked up the bottle to have a closer look. There, for anyone to see, was a tiny gold star.

'It *was* true,' Beth whispered to herself.

'I *did* sail on a pirate ship.' She shook her head and blinked her eyes and looked again. The gold star was still there. Maybe she'd tell Andy about it all later. He'd believe her. She didn't think anyone else would. Beth thought: We won't say a word about it to other people . . . it'll be our secret, Andy's and mine. She put the bottle with the *Crimson Cod* in it back on the table and went downstairs smiling to herself.

Later that morning, Beth's mother was tidying up her daughter's room. She found what looked like a doll's stocking on the floor beside the bed. It had been hand-knitted in thin stripes of purple and green. Beth's mum put it away in the dolls' house, wondering, not for the first time, where Beth found some of the things that ended up among her toys.

# The Box of Magic

## Malorie Blackman

It was Christmas Eve, but Peter was in no
hurry. His head bent, he dragged his feet
as he made his way slowly home. There was
no point in rushing. Mum and Dad would
only be arguing about something or other.
Peter and his sister Chloe had hoped that the
quarrelling would stop over Christmas. It
hadn't. If anything, it'd got worse.

Peter had spent all afternoon searching and

searching for the perfect present for his mum
and dad. Something that would stop them
quarrelling for just five minutes. Something
that would make Christmas the way it used
to be, with smiles and songs and happiness
in every corner of the house. But all the
searching had been for nothing. Peter didn't
have that much money to begin with and all
the things he could afford, he didn't want. All
the gifts he could afford looked so cheap and
tacky that Peter knew they would fall apart
about ten seconds after they were handled.
What was he going to do? He had to buy
something and time was running out.

Then he caught sight of it out of the
corner of his eye.

The medium-sized sign above the door
said 'The Christmas Shop' in spidery writing.
The small shop window was framed with
silver and gold tinsel and a scattering of glitter
like mini stars. At the bottom of the window,
fake snow had been sprayed. It looked so

much like the real thing that had it been outside the window instead of inside, Peter would've been sure it was real snow. A single Christmas tree laden with fairy lights and baubles and yet more tinsel stood proudly in the exact centre of the window.

Peter stood in front of the shop and stared. He'd never seen anything so . . . wonderful! It was as if Christmas had started in this shop and then spread out to cover the whole wide world.

'The Christmas Shop . . .' Peter muttered to himself.

He wondered why he'd never seen it before. True, it was behind the shopping precinct and he usually walked through the precinct not around it, but even so. Peter looked up and down the street. The few other shops in the same row as the Christmas Shop were all boarded up.

Unexpectedly, the shop door opened. A tall portly man with a white beard and a

merry twinkle
in his eyes
stood in the
doorway.

'Hello!
Come in!
Come in!' The
shopkeeper
beckoned.

'I . . .
er . . . don't
have much
money.' Peter
shook his
head.

'No matter.
Come in.' The
shopkeeper
turned and held the
door open. It was as if there was no doubt in
his mind that Peter would enter. Uncertainly,
Peter dithered on the pavement. He hadn't

intended to go in. He was only window-
shopping. But the shop looked so warm
and inviting and the shopkeeper seemed so
friendly. Peter walked into the shop.

And he gasped in amazement!

It was even better inside than it had
appeared from outside. It smelt of freshly
baked bread and warm cakes and toast and
cinnamon and nutmeg and it was so warm it
was as if the sun itself had come for a visit.

'Isn't my shop the best!' smiled the
shopkeeper. 'Look around. Feel free. You can
pick up anything, touch anything.'

Peter stared at the shopkeeper. He
certainly wasn't like any other shopkeeper
Peter had ever met. Usually shopkeepers
didn't like school kids in their shops and they
certainly didn't like them touching things.
Peter wandered around the shop, his dark
brown eyes wide with delight. Toys and
games and Christmas sweets and Christmas
treats filled every corner.

Peter's hand curled around the money in his pocket. He could buy all his Christmas presents in here. He bent his head to examine a gold and berry-red scarf. That would be perfect for his mum. And maybe the night-blue and yellow scarf for his dad. And he could get that little glass unicorn over there for Chloe. That was just the kind of thing she liked. The strange thing was, none of the items had prices on them.

'H-How much are these woolly scarves?' Peter asked, crossing his fingers in his pockets. 'And how much is that unicorn over there?'

'That depends on who they're for and why you think they'd like them,' answered the shopkeeper.

'The scarves are for my mum

29

and dad
and the
unicorn
is for my
sister. Chloe
likes things
made of glass. She
keeps them in her
bedroom on the
windowsill. And I
thought that Mum and Dad could have the
scarves to keep them warm.'

'And how much money do you have?'
asked the shopkeeper.

Peter took out all the money in his pocket.
The shopkeeper checked through it carefully.

'You're lucky,' said the shopkeeper.
'You've got enough for all the things you
want.'

'I have? Really?' Peter couldn't believe it.

The shopkeeper smiled and nodded.
Peter grinned at him, but slowly his smile

faded. He'd buy the scarves for his dad and
mum and then what? What good would
any present do? Peter could see it now:
Mum and Dad opening their presents on
Christmas Day.

'Thanks, Peter. That's great,' says Dad.

'Peter, that's wonderful,' says Mum.

And then they'd fling their presents to the
back of the chair and start shouting at each
other again.

'What's the matter, Peter?' asked the
shopkeeper gently.

Peter jumped. He'd been lost in a world of
his own.

'It's just that . . . Hang on a second. How
did you know my name?' Peter stared.

'It's a little game of mine,' the shopkeeper
beamed. 'I like to guess people's names and
nine times out of ten, I get it right.'

Peter was impressed.

'So you were saying?' the shopkeeper
prompted.

'I . . . I don't suppose you've got anything in your shop to stop my mum and dad fighting?' The moment the words were out of his mouth, Peter regretted it. What was he doing? He hadn't told anyone about his mum and dad, not even his best friend Andy. No one knew how things were at home except his sister Chloe and she didn't talk about it either.

'Oh, I see. Do your mum and dad argue a lot?' asked the shopkeeper.

'All the time,' Peter sighed.

The shopkeeper pursed his lips. 'Hmm! I think I have just the present you need – for your whole family.'

The shopkeeper went around his brightly coloured counter and disappeared down behind it. Moments later he straightened up, a huge smile on his face and a silver box in his hands.

'These are what you need,' he said.

'What are they?' Peter asked doubtfully.

'Christmas crackers,' announced the
shopkeeper proudly. At the disappointed look
on Peter's face, he added, 'Ah, they're not
just any crackers. They're magic. Guaranteed
to work or your money back.'

'How are they magic?' Peter asked suspiciously.

'The magic only works if they're pulled on Christmas Day, when you're all around the table eating dinner,' explained the shopkeeper.

'But how do they work?'

'It's hard to explain. You have to see the magic for yourself.'

'How much are they?' asked Peter, still doubtful.

Maybe he could buy them and still get the other presents as well.

'I'm afraid they're very expensive because they're magic,' said the shopkeeper. 'They'll cost you all the money you've got and even then I'm letting you have them cheap.'

Peter thought for a moment. Magic crackers. Crackers that would actually stop Mum and Dad from arguing. They were worth the money if they could do that. He took a deep breath.

'All right, I'll take them,' he said quickly, before he could change his mind.

Peter handed over his money and the shopkeeper handed over the box of eight crackers. Moments later, Peter was out of the shop and running all the way home. Magic crackers! He couldn't wait for Christmas Day.

'I've been in that kitchen since seven o'clock this morning. I think the least you could do is sit at the table with the rest of your family.' Mum's voice dripped with ice.

'I want to watch the end of this film,' Dad argued.

'Typical! You're so selfish,' Mum snapped.

Peter and Chloe looked at each other and sighed. Mum and Dad were at it again. Christmas Day – and they were still arguing.

'Dad, you and Mum and Chloe can open my present now,' Peter said desperately. 'The man in the Christmas Shop said they should only be opened when we're sitting round the table eating dinner.'

'Oh, all right then,' Dad grumbled.

'Oh, I see. You'll come to the table if Peter asks you to, but not if I ask you,' sniffed Mum.

'Peter doesn't nag me every two seconds,' Dad said as he sat down at the table.

Chloe shook her head and turned to look out of the window. Peter ran to get the present he'd bought. It was the only one left unopened under the tree. He stood between his mum and dad, putting the present down on the tablecloth. Mum and Dad looked at each other.

'Go on then,' Dad prompted.

'You do it,' said Mum.

'I'll do it,' said Chloe.

She tore off the bright red and yellow wrapping paper.

'It's a box of crackers,' she said, surprised.

'Not just any crackers,' Peter said eagerly. 'They're magic crackers!'

'Who told that you that?' Mum smiled.

'The man in the Christmas Shop,' Peter replied.

'Well, let's sit down. Then we can pull them and get on with our dinner,' said Dad, adding under his breath, 'And maybe then I can get back to my film.'

But the moment they all sat down, something peculiar began to happen. A strange feeling settled over the dinner table. A hopeful, expectant feeling – as if, in spite of themselves, everyone was waiting for something terrific, amazing and spectacular to happen all at once. The noise from the telly was just a distant hum at the other end of the room. Light like warm spring sunshine came from everyone smiling at everyone else as they watched Dad place two crackers beside each plate. Chloe held out her cracker to Dad. Peter held his Christmas cracker out to Mum.

'One! Two! Three!' they all shouted.

Bang! Pop! The sound of exploding crackers filled the room. Chloe and Peter got the biggest parts of the crackers. They peered down into them.

'They're . . . they're empty!' Chloe exclaimed.

'No! They can't be,' frowned Mum.

'See for yourself,' said Chloe, handing over her cracker.

Peter couldn't believe it. Empty . . . When he remembered the smiling, friendly face of the jolly man with the white beard in the Christmas Shop, he just couldn't believe it. That man wouldn't take his money and sell him a box of nothing – Peter was sure he wouldn't. And yet . . . and yet, his cracker was empty. Just an empty roll covered with some glossy paper and nothing else. No hats. No jokes. No gifts. Nothing.

'Maybe there were just two duff ones in the box,' Mum suggested.

Mum and Dad pulled their crackers next.

The same thing happened. They were empty.
Chloe and Peter pulled crackers five and six
at the same time as Mum and Dad pulled
crackers seven and eight.

They were all empty.

Peter examined each one, hoping against
hope that they'd got it wrong or it was a
trick – but it wasn't. He looked at Chloe,
then Mum and Dad – and burst into tears.
He couldn't help it.

'The shopkeeper told me they were magic
crackers,' Peter sobbed to Mum and Dad. 'I
only bought them because he said they would
make you stop arguing with each other. He
promised me they were magic. He promised
me . . .'

Dad stared. Mum's mouth fell open.'

'You . . . you bought them – because of
us?' Dad asked, aghast.

Peter sniffed and nodded.

'Never mind, Peter.' Chloe put her arm
around her younger brother's shoulder.

'Besides, nothing would stop Mum and Dad fighting. Not even a real box of magic crackers.' And with that, Chloe burst into tears too.

'Chloe! Peter!' Mum and Dad ran around the table to hug Peter and Chloe to them. 'We had no idea we were quarrelling that much.'

'And we had no idea we were upsetting both of you so much,' said Dad.

But Peter and Chloe couldn't stop crying.

'I'll tell you what,' said Mum. 'Let's make our own Christmas crackers. All this food will stay warm in the oven until we've finished.'

'Terrific idea.' Dad went over to the telly and switched it off. 'We'll make paper hats first,' Dad continued. 'Out of newspaper.'

Dad and Mum showed Peter and Chloe how to make sailor hats out of newspaper. They took about five minutes. Then they all sat down for dinner. Over dinner, everyone had to tell the worst jokes they knew, like,

'How do you make an apple puff? Chase it round the garden!' and 'Why did the elephant cross the road? Because it was the chicken's day off!' Dad's joke was 'Why did silly Billy stand on a ladder when he was learning to sing? So he could reach the high notes!' And Mum's joke was ancient but she was still proud of it! 'How do you make a Swiss Roll? Push him down a hill!' Chloe told a joke that Peter didn't get until Mum explained it. 'How do you tell how old a telephone is? Count its rings!' (Mum explained that you could tell the age of a tree by counting the rings through its trunk.) Everyone got Peter's joke. 'Why are vampires crazy? Because they're often bats!' And when everyone ran out of jokes, they made them up, which was even funnier!

After dinner when everyone was eating Christmas pudding, Mum grabbed Dad and whispered in his ear. Suddenly they both dashed off upstairs with the empty crackers.

Ten minutes later they reappeared with
the various ends of each cracker now glued
together.

'Cracker time!' said Mum. And she held
out a cracker to Chloe.

They both pulled.

'POP!' shouted Mum.

Chloe looked inside the
cracker and there was one of Mum's old
bangles – the gold and blue one which had
always been Chloe's favourite.

'Your turn,' said Dad, holding out
a cracker to Peter. They both shouted,
'BANG!'

Peter looked inside the cracker. There was
a pig made of Lego bricks. At least, that's
what Peter thought it was.

'It's not a pig. It's a rocket!'
said Dad, indignantly.

Mum started to giggle. 'I
told you it looked more like a
pig, dear,' she said.

They 'popped' the rest
of the crackers. They all
had very silly, very tacky,
wonderful presents in
them.

'Who needs rotten, mouldy
old crackers?' asked Dad. 'We can do it all
ourselves.'

'And they're much better too,' Mum
agreed. 'It's just a shame that Peter got
conned out of his money. Where did

you say the shop was?'

'Behind the precinct. All the other shops on the same street were boarded up,' Peter replied.

'There aren't any shops behind the precinct. The last one closed down over a year ago,' Dad frowned.

'There's one still open. It's called the Christmas Shop,' said Peter.

Mum and Dad looked at each other. They both shrugged.

'Never mind. I'd say they were the best crackers we've ever had,' smiled Mum. 'My jaw still aches from laughing at all those terrible jokes.'

'Those crackers were . . . a box of magic,' said Dad, giving Mum a cuddle.

Later that night, as Peter lay in bed, he still couldn't quite believe what had happened. Mum and Dad hadn't argued once since the crackers had been pulled. In fact it was

the most wonderful day they'd all had in a long, long time. The only cloud was the shopkeeper who'd sold Peter the crackers in the first place. Peter still didn't want to believe that the shopkeeper was a crook who had deliberately diddled him out of his money.

A strange tinkling-clinking came from across the room, followed by a plopping sound. Peter sat up and frowned. What was that? He switched on his bedside light. There it was again – the same strange noise. And it seemed to be coming from his chair by the window. Over the back of the chair were the jumper and the pair of trousers Peter had worn on Christmas Eve. That strange noise couldn't be coming from them – could it? Swallowing hard, Peter got up and tiptoed across to the chair.

Tinkle! Clinkle! Plop!

There it was again! Peter took a deep breath, counted to three, then quickly pulled the chair to one side. More money fell out of his trouser pockets and plopped on to the carpet. Peter's eyes goggled! Where had all the money come from? He scooped up the money on the floor, then picked up his trousers and dug into his pockets. There was more money inside there. He counted it all very carefully. It was the exact amount of money he had paid for the Christmas crackers . . .

Peter sat on his bed and stared down at the money in his hand. What was going on? He shook his head and looked around the room hoping for some clue. Had Mum and Dad done it? Had they put the money in his pockets to make up for him losing his money in the Christmas Shop? But they didn't know exactly how much he'd paid for the crackers. And now here he was, with the exact same coins in his hand.

Then something else caught his eye. There on his bedside table, were all the Christmas

cards he'd received from his friends. At the front was the card he'd got from his best friend Andy. Peter gasped and stared so hard, his eyes began to ache.

The face on the card . . .

Peter had seen that face before – in the Christmas Shop. The shopkeeper and Father Christmas were one and the same person! Peter picked up the card and studied it. The shopkeeper was Father Christmas. Peter was sure of it. And that would explain how he'd got his money back. Which meant only one thing . . .

The Christmas crackers were magic after all.

'Thank you,' Peter whispered to the Christmas card.

And he was sure that on the card, the smiling face of Father Christmas winked at him.

# The Christmas Truce

## Richmal Crompton

It was Hubert's mother's idea that the Outlaws versus Hubert Laneites feud should be abolished.

'Christmas, you know,' she said vaguely to William's mother, 'the season of peace and goodwill. If they don't bury the hatchet at this season they never will. It's so absurd for them to go on like this. Think how much *happier* they'd be if they were *friends*.'

Mrs Brown thought, murmured, 'Er –
yes,' uncertainly, and added, 'I've *tried*, you
know, but boys are so funny.'

'Yes,' said Mrs Lane earnestly (Mrs Lane
was large and breathless and earnest and
overdressed), 'but they're *very* sweet, aren't
they? Hubie's *awfully* sweet. I simply can't
think how anyone could quarrel with Hubie.
We'll make a *real* effort this Christmas to
put an end to this foolish quarrel, won't we?
I feel that if only your Willie got to know
my Hubie properly, he'd simply love him,
he would really. *Everyone* who really knows
Hubie loves him.'

Mrs Brown said, 'Er – yes,' still more
uncertainly, and Mrs Lane continued: 'I've
thought out how to do it. If you'll invite
Hubie to Willie's party, we'll *insist* on his
coming, and we'll invite Willie to Hubie's, and
you *insist* on his coming, and then it will be
all right. They'll have got to know each other,
and, I'm sure, learnt to love each other.'

Mrs Brown said, 'Er – yes,' more uncertainly than ever. She felt that Mrs Lane was being unduly optimistic, but still it *would* be nice to see the end of the feud that was always leading William into such wild and desperate adventures.

'Then we'll begin by—'

'Begin and end, my dear Mrs Brown,' said Mrs Lane earnestly, 'by making them attend each other's Christmas parties. I'm absolutely convinced that they'll *love* each other after that. I know anyway that Willie will love Hubie, because, when you really get to know Hubie, he's the most *lovable* boy you can possibly imagine.'

Mrs Brown said, 'Er – yes,' again, because she couldn't think of anything else to say, and so the matter was settled.

When it was broached to William, he was speechless with horror.

'*Him?*' he exploded fiercely when at last the power of speech returned to him. 'Ask

*him* to my Christmas party? I'd sooner not
have a Christmas party at all than ask *him*
to it. *Him!* Why, I wun't go to the *King's*
Christmas party, if *he* was going to be there.
Not if I had to be beheaded for it. *Him?*
Well, then I jolly well won't have a party at
all.'

But Mrs Brown was unexpectedly firm.
The overtures, she said, had come from
Hubert's mother, and they could not with
decency be rejected. It was the season of
peace and goodwill ('No one's ever peaceful
or goodwillin' to me at it,' put in William
bitterly); and we must all bury the hatchet
and start afresh.

'I don't want to bury no hatchet,' said
William tempestuously, ''cept in his head.
*Him!* Wantin' to come to my party! Cheek!'

But William's tempestuous fury was as
usual of no avail against his mother's gentle
firmness.

'It's no use, William,' she said. 'I've

51

*promised.* He's to come to your party, and you're to go to his, and Mrs Lane is quite sure that you'll be real friends after it.'

'*Me* friends with *him*!' exploded William. 'I'll never be friends with him 'cept in a lunatic asylum an'—'

'But William,' said his mother, stemming his flood of frenzied oratory, 'I'm sure he's a very nice little boy when you get to know him.'

William replied to this by a (partially) dumb and very realistic show of physical nausea.

But faced by the alternative of Hubert Lane and his friends as guests at his party or no party at all, William bowed to the inevitable.

'All right,' he said, 'I'll have him then an' – all right, I won't do anythin' to him or to any of them. I'll wait till it's all over. I'll wait till he's been to my party an' I've been to his, an' then – well, you'll be jolly sorry

you ever made us do it 'cause we'll have such a lot to make up.'

Mrs Brown, however, was content with her immediate victory. She sent an invitation to Hubert Lane and to Bertie Franks (Hubert's friend and lieutenant) and to Hubert's other friends, and they all accepted in their best copperplate handwriting. William and his Outlaws went about sunk deep in gloom.

'If it wasn't for the trifle an' the crackers,' said William darkly, 'I wouldn't have had it at all – not with *him*. An' it'll have to be a jolly fine trifle, practic'ly *all* cream, to make it worthwhile.'

His mood grew darker and darker as the day approached. He even discussed with his Outlaws the possibility of making a raid on the larder before the party, and carrying off trifles and jellies and fruit salad into the woods, leaving the Hubert Laneites to arrive and find the cupboard bare and their hosts flown. It was a tempting plan, but after dallying with it fondly for a few days they reluctantly gave it up, as being not really worth its inevitable consequences. Instead, they steeled themselves to go through the affair in the dogged spirit of martyrdom, their sufferings allayed only by the thought of the trifle and crackers, and the riot of hostilities that could take place as soon as the enforced Christmas truce was over. For the prospect of the end of the feud brought no glow of joy to the Outlaws' hearts. Without the Hubert Lane feud life would be dull indeed.

As the day of the party drew nearer, curiosity lightened the gloom of their spirits. How would the Hubert Laneites behave? Would they come reluctantly, surlily, at the bidding of authority, or would they come in a Christmas spirit of peace and goodwill, genuinely anxious to bury the hatchet? The latter possibility was too horrible to contemplate. Rather let them come in

the spirit in which one receives a deadly
foe in time of truce, all their thoughts and
energies centred on the happy moment when
hostilities might be resumed.

William, of course, could not watch
the preparations for his party and maintain
unbroken his pose of aloof displeasure. The
trifle was, he was convinced, the finest trifle
that had yet been seen in the neighbourhood;
there were jellies of every shape and hue,
there was a cream blancmange decorated
with cherries and angelica, and there was an
enormous iced Christmas cake. *And* there
were crackers. In the eyes of William and his
friends it was the crackers that lent the final
touch of festivity to the tea.

The Outlaws and their supporters, as
arranged, arrived first, and stood around
William like a bodyguard awaiting the
arrival of the Hubert Laneites. They wore
perfectly blank expressions, prepared to
meet the Hubert Laneites in whatever guise

they presented themselves. And the guise in which they ultimately presented themselves was worse than the Outlaws' worst fears. They were not surly foes, forced reluctantly to simulate neutrality, nor were they heralds of peace and goodwill. They advanced upon their host with an oily friendliness that was nauseating. They winked at each other openly. They said, 'Thanks *so* much for asking us, William. It was ripping of you. Oh, I say . . . what *topping* decorations!'

And they nudged each other and sniggered. William clenched his fists in his coat pockets and did swift mental calculations. His party would be over in four hours. In four days' time Hubert's party would come, and that would last about four hours, and then, *then*, THEN they would jolly well look out for themselves. The right hand that was clenched tightly in his coat for safety's sake was itching to plant itself firmly in Hubert's smug and smiling face. Mrs Brown, of course,

56

was deceived by their show of friendliness.

'There, William,' she whispered triumphantly, 'I knew it would be all right. They're so nice really, and *so* grateful to you for asking them. I'm sure you'll be the *greatest* friends after this. His mother *said* that he was a nice little boy.'

William did not reply to this because there wasn't anything that he could trust himself to say. He was still restraining himself with great difficulty from hurling himself upon his foes. They went in to tea.

'Oh, I say, how *ripping*! How *topping*!' said the Hubert Laneites gushingly to Mrs Brown, nudging each other and sniggering whenever her eye was turned away from them. Once Hubert looked at William and made his most challenging grimace, turning immediately to Mrs Brown to say with an ingratiating smile:

'It's a simply topping party, Mrs Brown, and it's awfully nice of you to ask us.'

Mrs Brown beamed at him and said:

'It's so nice to *have* you, Hubert,' and the other Hubert Laneites sniggered, and William kept his hands in his pockets with such violence that one of them went right through the lining. But the crowning catastrophe happened when they pulled the crackers.

Hubert went up to William, and said, 'See what I've got out of a cracker, William,' and held up a ring that sent a squirt of water into William's face. The Hubert Laneites went

into paroxysms of silent laughter. Hubert was all smirking contrition.

'I say, I'm so sorry, William, I'd no idea that it would do that. I'm frightfully sorry, Mrs Brown. I'd no idea that it would do that. I just got it out of one of the crackers. I say, I'm *so* sorry, William.'

It was evident to everyone but Mrs Brown that the ring had not come out of a cracker, but had been carefully brought by Hubert in order to play this trick on William. William was wiping water out of his eyes and ears.

'It's quite all right, dear,' said Mrs Brown. 'It was *quite* an accident, we all saw. They shouldn't have such nasty things in crackers, but it wasn't your fault. Tell him that you don't mind a bit, William.'

But William hastily left the room.

'Now let's go and have a few games, shall we?' said Mrs Brown.

Ginger followed William upstairs, and found him on the hearthrug in his bedroom, kneeling over a bolster that he was violently pummelling. Ginger knew that to William the bolster was not the bolster, but Hubert Lane's plump, well-nourished body. William raised a shining purple face from his task, and then the glow faded from it as he realized that the prostrate form before him was merely the bolster, and that Hubert Lane was triumphantly sniggering among his friends downstairs, not yet overtaken by Nemesis.

'Why don't you go down and smash his face in?' said Ginger simply.

William, returning reluctantly to Reality, raised the limp form of the bolster, and threw it on to the bed.

'Can't,' he said tersely, 'can't do anything not while he's in our house. I—'

'William, darling,' called his mother, 'come down, we're going to begin the games.'

William and Ginger went downstairs, and the rest of the party passed off uneventfully. The Hubert Laneites said goodbye at the end

with nauseous gratitude, and went sniggering down the drive.

'*There,* William!' said Mrs Brown, as she shut the door. 'I knew it would be all right. They were so grateful and they enjoyed it *so* much and you're *quite* friends now, aren't you?'

But William was already upstairs in his bedroom, pummelling his bolster with such energy that he burst his collar open.

During the days that intervened between William's party and Hubert Lane's party, the Hubert Laneites kept carefully out of the way of the Outlaws. Yet the Outlaws felt uneasily that something was brewing. Not content with scoring over them at William's party, Hubert meant to score over them in some way at his own. The Hubert Laneites looked upon the truce not as something that tied their hands for the time being, but as something that delivered their enemies into their power. William was uneasily aware that Hubert Lane would not feel the compunction that he had felt in the matter of his guests.

'We've gotter do somethin' to them at their party, same as they did to us at ours,' said Ginger firmly.

'Yes, but what can we do?' said William. 'We can't start fightin' 'em. We've promised not to. An' – an' there's nothin' else we *can* do. Jus' wait, jus' *wait* till their party's over.'

And William's fists curled themselves zestfully as he danced his most fiendish war dance in the middle of the road (his bolster had been so badly used lately that nearly all the feathers were coming out. Mrs Brown had asked him only that morning what on earth he was doing to it).

'But they'll never forget that water squirt,' said Ginger mournfully.

'Unless we do somethin' back,' said Douglas.

'What *can* we do in *their* house with them watchin' us all the time?' said Henry.

'We mus' jus' *think*,' said William, 'there's four days an' we'll think hard.'

But the day of Hubert's party arrived, and they'd thought of nothing. William looked downcast and spiritless. Even pummelling his bolster had lost its charm for him.

They met in the old barn in the morning to arrange their plan of action, but none of them could think of any plan of action to arrange, and the meeting broke up gloomily at lunchtime, without having come to any decision at all.

William walked slowly and draggingly through the village on his way home. His mother had told him to stop at the baker's with an order for her, and it was a sign of his intense depression that he remembered to do it. In ordinary circumstances William forgot his mother's messages in the village. He entered the baker's shop, and stared

around him resentfully. It seemed to be full of people. He'd have to wait all night before anyone took any notice of him. Just his luck, he reflected bitterly . . . Then he suddenly realized that the mountainous lady just in front of him was Mrs Lane. She was talking in a loud voice to a friend.

'Yes, Hubie's party is this afternoon. We're having William Brown and his friends. To put a stop to that silly quarrel that's gone on so long, you know. Hubie's so lovable that I simply can't think how anyone could quarrel with him. But, of course, it will be all right after today. We're having a Father Christmas, you know. Bates, our gardener, is going to be the Father Christmas and give out presents. I've given Hubie three pounds to get some *really* nice presents for it to celebrate the ending of the feud.'

William waited his turn, gave his message, and went home for lunch.

★

Immediately after lunch he made his way to Bates's cottage.

It stood on the road at the end of the Lanes' garden. One gate led from the garden to the road, and the other from the garden to the Lanes' shrubbery. Behind the cottage was Bates's treasured kitchen garden, and at the bottom was a little shed where he stored apples. The window of the shed had to be open for airing purposes, but Bates kept a sharp lookout for his perpetual and inveterate enemies: boys.

William approached the cottage with great circumspection, looking anxiously around to be sure that none of the Hubert Laneites were in sight. He had reckoned on the likelihood of their all being engaged in preparation for the party.

He opened the gate, walked up the path and knocked at the door, standing poised on one foot ready to turn to flee should Bates, recognizing him and remembering some of his former exploits in his kitchen garden, attack him on sight. He heaved a sigh of relief, however, when Bates opened the door. It was clear that Bates did not recognize him. He received him with an ungracious scowl, but that, William could see, was because he was *a* boy, not because he was *the* boy.

'Well?' said Bates sharply, holding the door open a few inches, 'what d'you want?'

William assumed an ingratiating smile, the smile of a boy who has every right to demand admittance to the cottage.

'I say,' he said with a fairly good imitation of the Hubert Laneites' most patronizing manner, 'you've got the Father Christmas things here, haven't you?'

The ungraciousness of Bates's scowl did not relax, but he opened the door a few inches wider in a resigned fashion. He had been pestered to death over the Father Christmas things. These boys had been in and out of his cottage all day with parcels

and whatnot, trampling over his doorstep and 'mussing up' everything. He'd decided some time ago that it wasn't going to be worth the five shillings that Mrs Lane was giving him for it. He took for granted that William was one of the Hubert Laneites coming once more to 'muss up' his bag of parcels, and take one out or put one in, or snigger over them as they'd been doing every day for the last week. But he *did* think that they'd have left him in peace on the very afternoon of the party.

'Yes,' he said surlily, 'I've got the things 'ere an' they're all right, so there's no call to start upsettin' of 'em again. I've had enough of you comin' in an' mussin' the place up.'

'I only wanted to count them, and make sure that we've got the right number,' said William with an oily friendliness that was worthy of Hubert himself.

The man opened the door with a shrug.

'All right,' he said, 'go in and count 'em.

I tell you, I'm sick of the whole lot of you,
I am. Mussin' the place up. Look at your
boots!'

William looked at his boots, made an
ineffectual attempt to wipe them on the
mat, and entered the cottage. He had an
exhilarating sense of danger and adventure as
he entered. At any minute he might arouse
the man's suspicions. His ignorance of where
the presents were, for instance, when he was
supposed to have been visiting them regularly,
might give him away completely. Moreover,
a Hubert Laneite might arrive any minute
and trap him in the cottage. It was, in short,
a situation after William's own heart. The
immediate danger of discovery was averted by
Bates himself, who waved him irascibly into
the back parlour, where the presents were
evidently kept. William entered, and threw a
quick glance out of the window. Yes, Ginger
was there, as they had arranged he should be,
hovering near the shed where the apples were

sorted. Then he looked round the room. A red cloak and hood and white beard were spread out on the sofa, and on the hearthrug lay a sackful of small parcels.

'Well, count 'em for goodness' sake an' let's get a bit of peace,' said Bates more irritably than ever. William fell on his knees and began to make a pretence of counting the parcels. Suddenly he looked up and gazed out of the window.

'I say!' he said, 'there's a boy taking your apples.'

Bates leapt to the window. There, upon the roof of the shed, was Ginger, with an arm through the open window, obviously in the act of purloining apples and carefully exposing himself to view.

With a yell of fury Bates sprang to the door and down the path towards the shed. He had forgotten everything but this outrage upon his property. Left alone, William turned his attention quickly to the sack. It contained

the parcels, each one labelled and named.
He had to act quickly. Bates had set off after
Ginger, but he might return at any minute.
Ginger's instructions were to lure him on by

keeping just out of reach, but Bates might
tire of the chase before they'd gone a few
yards, and, remembering his visitor, return to
the cottage in order to prevent his 'mussin''
things up any more than necessary. William
had no time to investigate. He had to act
solely upon his suspicions and his knowledge
of the characters of Hubert and his friends.
Quickly he began to change the labels of
the little parcels, putting the one marked
William on to the one marked Hubert, and
exchanging the labels of the Outlaws and
their supporters for those of the Hubert
Laneites and their supporters. Just as he was
fastening the last one, Bates returned, hot and
breathless.

'Did you catch him?' said William, secure
in the knowledge that Ginger had outstripped
Bates more times than any of them could
remember.

'Naw,' said Bates, panting and furious. 'I'd
like to wring his neck. I'd larn him if I got

hold of him. Who was he? Did you see?'

'He was about the same size as me,' said William in the bright, eager tone of one who is trying to help, 'or he may have been just a *tiny* bit smaller.'

Bates turned upon him as if glad of the chance to vent his irascibility upon somebody.

'Well, you clear out,' he said. 'I've had enough of you mussin' the place up, an' you can tell the others that they can keep away too. An' I'll be glad when it's over, I tell you. I'm sick of the lot of you.'

Smiling the patronizing smile that he associated with the Hubert Laneites, William took a hurried departure, and ran home as quickly as he could. He found his mother searching for him despairingly.

'Oh, William, where *have* you been? You ought to have begun to get ready for the party *hours* ago.'

'I've just been for a walk,' said William casually. 'I'll be ready in time all right.'

72

With the unwelcome aid of his mother, he was ready in time, spick and span and spruce and shining.

'I'm so *glad* that you're friends now and that that silly quarrel's over,' said Mrs Brown as she saw him off. 'You feel much *happier* now that you're friends, don't you?'

William snorted sardonically, and set off down the road.

The Hubert Laneites received the Outlaws with even more nauseous friendliness than they had shown at William's house. It was evident, however, from the way they sniggered and nudged each other that they had some plan prepared. William felt anxious. Suppose that the plot they had so obviously prepared had nothing to do with the Father Christmas . . . Suppose that he had wasted his time and trouble that morning . . . They went into the hall after tea, and Mrs Lane said roguishly:

'Now, boys, I've got a visitor for you.'

Immediately Bates, inadequately disguised as Father Christmas and looking fiercely resentful of the whole proceedings, entered with his sack. The Hubert Laneites sniggered delightfully. This was evidently the crowning moment of the afternoon. Bates took the parcels out one by one, announcing the name on each label.

The first was William.

The Hubert Laneites watched him go up to receive it in paroxysms of silent mirth. William took it and opened it, wearing a sphinx-like expression. It was the most magnificent mouth organ that he had ever seen. The mouths of the Hubert Laneites dropped open in horror and amazement. It was evidently the present that Hubert had destined for himself. Bates called out Hubert's name. Hubert, his mouth still hanging open with horror and amazement, went to receive his parcel. It contained a short pencil with shield and rubber of the sort that can be

purchased for a penny or twopence.

He went back to his seat blinking. He examined his label. It bore his name. There was no mistake about it. William was thanking Mrs Lane effusively for his present.

'Yes, dear,' she was saying, 'I'm so glad you like it. I haven't had time to look at them but I told Hubie to get nice things.'

Hubert opened his mouth to protest, and then shut it again. He was beaten and he knew it. He couldn't very well tell his mother that he'd spent the bulk of the money on the presents for himself and his particular friends, and had spent only a few coppers on the Outlaws' presents. He couldn't think what had happened. He'd been so sure that it would be all right. The Outlaws would hardly have had the nerve publicly to object to their presents, and Mrs Lane was well meaning but conveniently short-sighted, and took for granted that everything that Hubie did was perfect.

Hubert sat staring at his pencil and blinking his eyes in incredulous horror. Meanwhile the presentation was gong on. Bertie Franks's present was a ruler that could not have cost more than a penny, and Ginger's was a magnificent electric torch. Bertie stared at the torch with an expression that would have done credit to a tragic mask, and Ginger hastened to establish his permanent right to his prize by going up to thank Mrs Lane for it.

'Yes, it's lovely, dear,' she said, 'I told Hubie to get nice things.'

Douglas's present was a splendid penknife, and Henry's a fountain pen, while the corresponding presents for the Hubert Laneites were an India rubber and a notebook. The Hubert Laneites watched their presents passing into the enemies' hands with expressions of helpless agony. But Douglas's parcel had more than a penknife in it. It had a little bunch of imitation flowers with an India-rubber bulb attached with a tiny label, 'Show this to

William and press the rubber thing.' Douglas
took it to Hubert. Hubert knew it, of course,
for he had bought it, but he was paralysed
with horror at the whole situation.

'Look, Hubert,' said Douglas.

A fountain of ink caught Hubert
neatly in the eye. Douglas was all surprise
and contrition.

'I'm so sorry, Hubert,' he said, 'I'd no idea that it was going to do that. I've just got it out of my parcel and I'd no idea that it was going to do that. I'm so sorry, Mrs Lane. I'd no idea that it was going to do that.'

'Of course you hadn't, dear,' said Mrs Lane. 'It's Hubie's own fault for buying a thing like that. It's very foolish of him indeed.'

Hubert wiped the ink out of his eyes and sputtered helplessly.

Then William discovered that it was time to go.

'Thank you so much for our lovely presents, Hubert,' he said politely, 'we've had a *lovely* time.'

And Hubert, under his mother's eye, smiled a green and sickly smile.

The Outlaws marched triumphantly down the road, brandishing their spoils. William was playing on his mouth organ, Ginger was flashing his electric light, Henry waving his

fountain pen, and Douglas slashing at the hedge with his penknife.

Occasionally they turned round to see if their enemies were pursuing them, in order to retrieve their treasures.

But the Hubert Laneites were too broken in spirit to enter into open hostilities just then.

As they walked, the Outlaws raised a wild and inharmonious paean of triumph.

And over the telephone Mrs Lane was saying to Mrs Brown:

'Yes, dear, it's been a complete success. They're the *greatest* friends now. I'm sure it's been a Christmas that they'll all remember all their lives.'

# Princess Mirror-Belle:
# The Sleepwalking Beauty

## Julia Donaldson

Christmas pudding or Sleeping Beauty? That was the question Ellen was asking herself as she wrapped up a present for her best friend Katy.

It was Christmas Eve, and Katy was having a fancy dress party. Ellen couldn't decide what to go as. She had already worn the Christmas pudding costume in the end-of-term ballet show. It had a wire frame which was quite

uncomfortable and meant you couldn't sit down. Still, it did look good, especially the little cap with the sprig of holly on it.

The Sleeping Beauty costume wasn't so Christmassy. It was just a lacy white Victorian nightdress Ellen's mother had bought at a car-boot sale. But it was very pretty, and Ellen decided to wear it if she could find something else to go with it.

As soon as she had finished wrapping up the present she tried on the nightdress. Looking through her dressing-up box she found an old net curtain which she draped over her head. She fixed it into place with a gold-coloured plastic headband which looked quite like a crown. There was a pair of very long white button-up gloves in the box too. Mum had told her that her great-grandmother used to wear them for going to balls. Ellen put them on and then went to see how the whole outfit looked in her wardrobe mirror.

She should have known better, of course.

'I don't see why *you* need to bother with gloves,' came a voice from the mirror. Ellen knew that this wasn't her reflection talking; it was Princess Mirror-Belle. Mirror-Belle looked just like Ellen but her character was very different, and she had a habit of appearing at all the wrong times.

Mirror-Belle looked at Ellen critically from the mirror. 'There's really no need for those gloves,' she said. 'After all, it wouldn't really matter if you pricked your finger.'

Ellen was dismayed. 'Oh, Mirror-Belle, this isn't a good time to come!' she said.

'What do you mean?' said Mirror-Belle, looking offended. 'Surely you'd rather play with a princess than by yourself?'

'But I'm not going to be by myself. I'm just off to Katy's party. This is my Sleeping Beauty costume.'

Mirror-Belle laughed. 'Poor you, having to

dress up as Sleeping Beauty, when I really am one,' she said.

'No you're not – you're Mirror-Belle.'

'Of course – and "Belle" means "Beauty". I thought everyone knew that. Have you forgotten what I told you the very first time we met?'

Ellen thought back. She did seem to remember some story about Mirror-Belle's wicked fairy godmother pricking her finger and sending her to sleep for a very long time. But then Mirror-Belle was always telling her stories and Ellen never knew how many of them were true.

Mirror-Belle had stepped out of the mirror and was looking round Ellen's bedroom. Her eyes fell on the cap belonging to the Christmas pudding costume.

'It's very careless of you to leave that holly lying around,' she said. 'Suppose I pricked my finger on it?'

'It's not real holly,' said Ellen. 'It's just

made of plastic. And I don't know what you're so worried about. I thought you'd already gone to sleep for a hundred years.'

'Two hundred,' Mirror-Belle corrected her. 'So what?'

'Well, you woke up in the end, didn't you? So the spell must be broken.'

'You obviously don't know my wicked fairy godmother,' said Mirror-Belle. 'I'm in danger every day of my life. The next time I prick my finger it's going to happen all over again, only this time it could be for three hundred years. That's why I always wear gloves.'

Ellen was sure she hadn't ever seen Mirror-Belle wearing gloves before, but she didn't want to start arguing about that now. 'Well, anyway, Mirror-Belle, the party will be starting soon. I'll have to go.'

'Don't you mean "We"?' asked Mirror-Belle, looking offended again.

'No, I don't. I'm sorry, but it would

all be too complicated. Everyone would keep thinking you were me, or my twin or something, and I'm just not in the mood for that.'

'Aha!' Mirror-Belle flipped her net curtain over her head so that it hid her face like a veil. 'Now all your problems are solved!' she said.

Ellen doubted it, but she realized she couldn't win. 'Oh, all right then. But we can't both wear the same costume. I'll have to be a Christmas pudding after all.'

★

Ellen put her finger to her lips as they went downstairs. Her mother didn't believe Princess Mirror-Belle existed and now didn't seem the best time for her to meet her.

Mum had invited some of her piano pupils round to play Christmas carols to each other, and at the moment Robert Rumbold was hammering out 'Silent Night', though it sounded more like 'Very Loud Night'.

Katy's house was just round the corner. Her dad opened the door to Ellen and Mirror-Belle.

'Oh good, the food's arrived,' he joked when he saw Ellen dressed as a Christmas pudding. 'I hope they put a lot of brandy in you.' He turned to Mirror-Belle. 'And I suppose this delicious-looking white creation is the Christmas cake.'

Ellen laughed politely, and then blushed when Mirror-Belle said in a haughty voice, 'Please tell the lady of the house that the royal

guest has arrived.' She seemed to think that she was speaking to the butler.

Luckily Katy's father thought this was a great joke. 'Katy! The princess and the pudding are here!' he called out. Then, 'If you'll excuse me, I'd better pop upstairs and get changed,' he said to Ellen and Mirror-Belle.

'Yes, you do look a bit scruffy. And don't forget to give your shoes a polish while you're at it,' said Mirror-Belle.

Before Ellen could tick her off, Katy arrived, dressed as a reindeer.

'I've brought Mirror-Belle with me. I hope that's all right,' said Ellen.

'Of course it is.' Katy had already met Mirror-Belle once, when she had appeared at their school, and looked pleased to see her again. She took them both into the sitting room, where various children in fancy dress were chattering and eating crisps.

'What an extraordinary-looking tree,' said

Mirror-Belle. 'Why is it growing indoors?'

'It's a Christmas tree,' said Ellen.

Mirror-Belle was still bewildered. 'What is this Christmas thing that everyone keeps talking about? Is it some kind of disease?'

Katy laughed. 'No, of course not. Why do you think that?'

'Well, that tree looks diseased to me. Half the needles have fallen off it, and the fruits are gleaming in a most unhealthy-looking way. I think you should take it back to the forest immediately.'

'They're not fruits, they're fairy lights,' said Ellen.

'I think I'm the expert on fairies round here, and I've never heard of such a thing,' said Mirror-Belle.

Katy's mother came in. 'There's just time for one game before tea,' she said.

She handed out pencils and paper and then showed them all a bag. 'There are five different things inside here. You'll all get a

88

turn to feel them and then write down what
you think they are.'

'I can't possibly risk that,' objected Mirror-
Belle. 'Supposing there's something sharp in
there? I might prick my finger. But I like the
idea of tea. Perhaps you could call one of
your servants and ask them to bring me mine
while the rest of you play this game.'

Katy's mother told her that she would
have to wait and have tea with the others.
'But I promise you there's nothing sharp in
the bag. Why don't you join in?'

Reluctantly Mirror-Belle agreed, though
she refused to take her gloves off.

'This is easy,' she said when it was her turn
to feel inside the bag, and she began writing
furiously.

'You can read out your list first if you
like, Mirror-Belle,' said Katy's mother when
everyone was ready.

'Very well,' said Mirror-Belle. 'There's
some mermaid's hair, a wishing ring, an

invisibility pill, a witch's eyeball and a tool for removing stones from a unicorn's hoof.'

Everyone laughed.

'Very imaginative,' said Katy's mum. 'I'll give you a mark for the pill, though I don't think it has any magic powers; it's just an ordinary aspirin.'

Ellen had written, 'seaweed, ring pull from drink can, pill, grape and matchstick', and was delighted to find that she was the only one to get them all right. Her prize was a meringue snowman.

At teatime there were crackers to pull. Mirror-Belle refused to put on the paper crown inside hers and told everyone about the different crowns she had back home.

'Why are you wearing that veil thing?' someone asked.

'It's because my face is so beautiful that you might fall down dead if you saw it,' replied Mirror-Belle. Then she kept them entertained with stories about life in the

palace. Ellen was glad that the other children seemed to like Mirror-Belle and think she was fun.

It was after tea that the trouble started. When everyone was back in the sitting room, Katy's mother peeped round the door and announced, 'He's coming!'

'Ho ho ho!' came a loud laugh and in strode Father Christmas. Ellen felt quite excited, even though Katy had told her that it was really just her dad dressed up.

'Merry Christmas, boys and girls!' said Father Christmas. 'Happy holidays! Ho ho ho!'

'You're extremely late,' Mirror-Belle told him. 'All the food's gone already.'

'Ho ho ho!' laughed Father Christmas, even louder than before.

'What so funny?' asked Mirror-Belle.

Father Christmas took no notice of her. Still laughing, he heaved the sack off his back. 'It's nice to see you all so wide awake!' he

91

told the children. 'When I come down your chimneys you're always fast asleep. It gets a bit lonely sometimes.'

Mirror-Belle had been looking puzzled but now her face cleared. 'So *that's* who you are – that burglar character!' she said.

One or two children laughed but the others said 'Shh' or 'Shut up'.

Father Christmas took a present out of his sack. 'Now then, who's been good all year?' he asked.

'Me!' they all shouted.

He beckoned to a girl dressed as a star and she came shyly forward.

'You look a bit of a star! Ho ho ho!' Father

Christmas handed her the present and she unwrapped it. It was a box of soaps shaped like robins.

'Thank you,' said the star girl, looking really pleased.

Ellen glanced at Mirror-Belle and thought that she still looked suspicious, though it was hard to tell through the net veil.

Father Christmas gave a torch to a boy dressed as a cracker, and a card game to one in a Batman costume.

'Excuse me, but are you quite sure these things are yours to give away?' Mirror-Belle asked him.

'Ho ho ho,' replied Father Christmas, but Ellen didn't think he sounded quite so jolly as before. He beckoned to Mirror-Belle, perhaps hoping that once she had a present of her own she would stop pestering him.

'Now then, Your Royal Highness, let's find something special for you,' he said.

Mirror-Belle gave him half a smile. 'At

least you know how to address me,' she said. But when she opened her present her face fell.

'What are these supposed to be?' she asked, looking at the five little felt objects she had unwrapped.

Father Christmas didn't look too sure himself, so Ellen came to the rescue. 'They're finger puppets,' she said. 'A reindeer and a robin and a snowman and a Christmas tree and Father Christmas. They're lovely, aren't they, Mirror-Belle?'

But Mirror-Belle didn't think so. 'Is this a trick to get me to take off my gloves?' she asked Father Christmas. 'Well, I'm not going to, but I think you should take off your socks and shoes.'

'Mirror-Belle! Stop it!' said Ellen, but the Batman boy was intrigued. 'Why should he?' he asked.

'They're stolen!' said Mirror-Belle. 'They belong to the butler who opened the door.'

94

'There isn't a butler,' said someone, and, 'She means Katy's dad,' said someone else.

'Well, whoever he was, he was wearing scruffy black shoes and socks with green-and-brown diamonds up the sides. Don't you remember, Ellen?' said Mirror-Belle.

'Now, now, you've had your bit of fun,' said Father Christmas, covering up his shoes with the hem of his robe and trying to sound jolly again. 'Let someone else have a turn, eh? Ho ho ho!'

But Mirror-Belle ignored him. 'I see it all now!' she said. 'The butler person told Ellen and me he was going upstairs to get changed, and I ordered him to polish his shoes. He must have taken them off, and his socks too. Then I suppose he must have had a little nap, and meanwhile this burglar came down the chimney and stole them.'

She turned to Katy's mother. 'Aren't you going to phone the police?'

'No,' said Katy's mother, 'but I think

95

perhaps we'd better phone your parents and tell them you're getting a bit too excited.'

'Of course I'm excited!' cried Mirror-Belle. 'It's not every day you catch a crook red-handed. Look! He's even got a false beard!' She reached out and tried to tug it, but Father Christmas dodged out of the way.

'Now now, I'm beginning to wonder if you really are a good little girl,' he said. 'Maybe I'd better fill your stocking with coal instead of presents?'

Mirror-Belle looked horrified. 'You're not filling any of my stockings with anything!' she said. 'In fact, if you come anywhere near the palace I'll set my dog, Prince Precious Paws, on you. And you'd better not try going down my friend Ellen's chimney either.'

'Of course I'll go down Ellen's chimney; she's a good girl, and I've got a little something for her here,' said Father Christmas, beckoning to Ellen.

Ellen came up to receive her present. 'Do

calm down, Mirror-Belle,' she pleaded.

'I know!' said Katy. 'We're going to play hide-and-seek next. Why don't you go and hide now, Mirror-Belle? I bet you'll find a really good placc.'

Mirror-Belle sighed. 'Very well, since no one here will listen to reason,' she said, and she flounced out of the room.

Later, when all the presents had been given out and Father Christmas had said goodbye, the other children went to look for Mirror-Belle. Ellen was not surprised when they couldn't find her.

'It's all right,' she told Katy's mum. 'I think she must have gone home. She quite often does that.' She didn't add that the way Mirror-Belle went home was through a mirror.

Ellen thought she would never get to sleep. Christmas Eve was always like that. Her empty stocking (really one of Dad's thick

mountain-climbing socks) lay limply on the bottom of her bed. In the morning it would be fat and knobbly with presents, and this was just one of the exciting thoughts that was keeping her awake.

'But I did get to sleep all the other years, so I will tonight,' she told herself, and in the end she must have drifted off.

A rapping sound woke her and she sat up in bed. The room was dark. It was still night.

She wriggled her toes. Yes! From the lovely heaviness on top of them she knew that her stocking was full. But why was her heart thumping so hard? It didn't feel just like nice Christmassy excitement. That noise had scared her. What was it?

Mum and Dad liked Ellen to take her stocking into their room, so that they could watch her open it. This year she had decided to take them in a cup of tea as well. But somehow she knew it was too early for that. She switched on her lamp and looked at the

clock beside her bed. Only four thirty.

Suddenly she heard another rap. It was coming from the skylight window. Ellen wished now that Mirror-Belle hadn't gone on about burglars so much, because that was the first thing she thought of. It sounded as if someone was trying to break into her bedroom.

'Ellen! Let me in!'

That hoarse whisper didn't belong to a burglar. It was Princess Mirror-Belle.

For once Ellen was relieved to see her face, which was pressed against the skylight window.

'I'm coming!' she said and got out of bed. The window was in the sloping part of Ellen's ceiling, where it came down so low that grown-ups couldn't stand up properly. Ellen didn't even need to climb on a chair to open it.

Princess Mirror-Belle landed on the floor with a thump. She didn't look much like Sleeping Beauty any more. Her face was dirty, her hair wild and her nightdress torn. In one hand she clutched the now grubby veil.

'Mirror-Belle! I thought you'd gone back through one of Katy's mirrors!'

'What, and leave you unprotected? Is that the kind of friend you think I am?'

'I don't know what you mean. Oh, Mirror-Belle, you're shivering! Why don't you get into my bed?'

'That's a good idea.'

When the two girls were sitting up in bed together, snugly covered by Ellen's duvet, Ellen said, 'What were you doing on the roof? And how did you get there?'

'I climbed up that creeper at the side of your house. Very useful things, creepers. I'm sure my friend Rapunzel wishes that there had been one growing up the tower that horrible witch locked her up in for all those years. Then the prince could have climbed up that instead of up her hair. I must say, I wouldn't let any old prince climb up my hair, even if it was long enough. A lot of

Rapunzel's hair fell out after that, you know, and it's never been the same since.'

'Oh, Mirror-Belle, do stop going on about Rapunzel and tell me what you've been up to.'

'This,' said Mirror-Belle, and she spread out the grubby veil which she had been clutching. Something was written on it in big black letters.

'I had to use a lump of coal for the writing, but it looks quite good, I think. Don't you?'

Ellen was getting quite good at reading Mirror-Belle's backwards writing so she didn't need to hold it up to the mirror to see that it said, 'Go Away, Father Christmas'.

'I spread it out on the roof and sat on the chimney pot all night,' said Mirror-Belle triumphantly. 'I'm pretty sure that's done the trick. I don't think he'll come now.'

'Er . . .' Ellen couldn't help glancing down at the bulgy stocking on her bed, and Mirror-Belle spotted it too.

'Good heavens! He's craftier than I thought. How on earth did he get in? You'd better check all your belongings immediately, Ellen, and see what he's stolen.'

'I'm sure he hasn't stolen anything,' said Ellen.

Mirror-Belle glanced round the room suspiciously and then at the stocking again.

'I notice there isn't one for me,' she said. 'That's a relief,' she added, though in fact she sounded disappointed.

Ellen thought quickly and said, 'I've got something for you, Mirror-Belle. Close your eyes for a minute.'

Mirror-Belle looked pleased, and Ellen

hastily wrapped up the present that Father
Christmas had given her at Katy's party.

'You can open them now.'

Mirror-Belle unwrapped the present, and
gazed in delight at the little glass dome with a
forest scene of deer and trees inside it.

'Give it a shake,'
said Ellen. Mirror-
Belle shook it, and
snowflakes rose up
and whirled around.

'This is just what
I've always wanted,'
she said. Ellen had
never heard her sound
so happy about anything
before and felt glad she
had thought of giving her the
snowstorm, even though she really liked it
herself.

After a few more shakes and smiles,
Mirror-Belle started eyeing Ellen's stocking

again. 'I hope it isn't full of coal,' she said.

'I'm sure it's not.'

'Let's just check.'

'But I usually open it in Mum and Dad's room, and it's too early to wake them.'

'I still think we have a duty to investigate,' said Mirror-Belle grandly.

'Well . . .' Ellen was beginning to waver. After all, it was so hard to wait. 'I know, let's just open one thing each and then wrap them up again.'

She gave Mirror-Belle a cube-shaped parcel and unwrapped a long thin one herself.

'Cool! It's a fan. What's in yours?'

'It's a little box.' Mirror-Belle opened it and inside was a brooch shaped like a Scottie dog. 'Hmm, not a patch on any of my own jewellery, but quite amusing all the same,' she said. 'Would you like me to fasten it on to your pyjama top?'

'Yes, please,' said Ellen.

Suddenly Mirror-Belle gave a little scream.

104

'What's the matter?'

'I've pricked my finger!'

'Oh dear.' Ellen looked at the finger which was sticking out of a hole in the dirty white glove. She couldn't see any blood or even a pinprick. 'I'm sure you'll be all right,' she said.

'No, I won't. I feel sleepy already.'

'Oh help! Is there anything I can do?'

'No, nothing at all, but don't worry. It's quite a nice feeling actually. In fact, I think I probably *need* a three-hundred-year sleep after all the adventures I've had recently.'

Mirror-Belle gave a huge yawn and lay down in Ellen's bed.

'No! You can't go to sleep here!'

But Mirror-Belle's eyes were already closed, and she began to snore gently.

'Wake up, Mirror-Belle!' Ellen was shouting now.

'Ellen! What's going on!' she heard her mother's voice call.

Ellen looked at the clock. It was half past

five – still a bit earlier than her parents liked to be disturbed, but it seemed that she had woken them up already.

Well, she decided, at least now she could prove to them once and for all that Mirror-Belle really existed. If she was going to stay asleep in Ellen's bed for three hundred years there could be no doubt about that.

'Happy Christmas,' said Mum sleepily, and then, 'Oh, how lovely,' when she saw that Ellen had brought her and Dad a cup of tea.

'Where's your stocking?' asked Dad.

'It's upstairs still, and so is Mirror-Belle! You've got to come and see her.'

Mum sighed. 'Honestly, Ellen, can't we even get a break from Mirror-Belle on Christmas Day?'

'But she's asleep in my bed! Please, Mum – please come!'

Mum yawned. 'Let us drink our tea first,' she said. 'You go back up and we'll come

in a couple of minutes.'

'All right.' After all, Ellen thought, there was no hurry.

But when she got back to her bedroom she found that Mirror-Belle was no longer in the bed. She was walking slowly across the room with her arms stretched in front of her.

'Mirror-Belle! Have you woken up already?'

'No, of course not, silly. I'm sleepwalking,' said Mirror-Belle. Ellen noticed that she was grasping the snowstorm in her right hand. She had reached the wardrobe now.

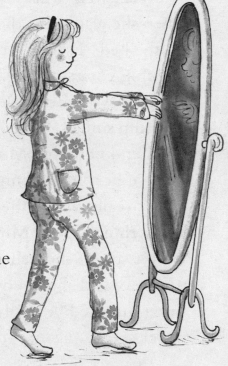

'Goodbye, Ellen,' she said in a strange calm voice and disappeared into the mirror.

'Mirror-Belle! Come back!' Ellen called into the mirror, but it was her own reflection and not Mirror-Belle that she saw there.

'All right then, where's this sleeping princess?' said Dad, coming into the room with Mum.

'You've just missed her,' said Ellen. 'She's sleepwalked into the mirror.'

'Well, well, what a surprise,' said Mum. Then she glanced at the wrapping paper on the bed. 'I see you couldn't wait to start opening your stocking.'

'That was Mirror-Belle's idea,' said Ellen.

Mum smiled. 'Of course,' she said.

Ellen knew that Mum and Dad didn't believe her. It was annoying, but she didn't really blame them. There were quite a few things about Mirror-Belle that she wasn't sure if she believed herself. For instance, had she really gone to sleep for three hundred years? If so, Ellen would never see her again – unless she did some

more sleepwalking, that is.

'Well,' said Mum, 'are you going to bring your stocking downstairs now?'

'Yes,' said Ellen. Suddenly she felt excited all over again.

Mirror-Belle had gone, but Christmas Day had only just begun.

# The Witness

Robert Westall

A great wind blew out of Asia; from that
finger of ice that would one day be
called Everest. It thundered across white
Steppes, and disturbed the King of Parthia's
slumbers. Cyrenius, Governor of Syria, tossed
and turned, worrying about the Egyptian
furniture, shipped to Rome three days before.

Across the desert the wind blew icy and
dry. But when it reached the warmth of Judea

it dropped flurries of snow. One of them caught the cat as she reached the crest of the stable roof. She crouched wretched: the wind blowing her fur into wild saucers, exposing points of warm, pink, vulnerable skin. She spat into the wind's face in helpless fury.

Her misery was total. She was heavy with kitten. In this her first year of exile, she was unprepared for the Judean cold. Worse, she couldn't find a dark private place to give birth. Turned out of cellar and byre by servants putting down straw and blankets for extra guests. Strangers everywhere.

Egypt had been so different: basking in the sun on the temple terrace; dabbling for fish in the green waters of the temple canal; the manicured hands of the priests, who thought it a prayer to stroke her. The common people would hold back the carts while she stepped past. In Egypt, she was a goddess, the spirit of Bastet-Ra, Mother of the Sacred Trinity, cat-goddess of Bubastis by the Nile. Parents would sell the hair of their children to bring her offerings, watch with bated breath as she washed, counting the number of times her paw crossed her ear, believing that this foretold the future.

This stable was her last hope. Leaking roof, flaking mud walls that let in draughts, old straw full of the smells of other animals. But better than nothing. If she gave birth in the open, the wind would kill the kittens before morning.

She leapt to the ground, with a sickening grunt. Yet even in her wretchedness she was graceful. Golden, long-legged, huge-eared.

In the doorway, she spat again. People even here; poor people too, from the smell. Rich strangers were sometimes well enough. Their perfumes reminded her of the temple. They might stroke her, feed her from their own rich food bowls; but poor people drove her out with shouts and blows . . .

She still couldn't understand why her

world had changed. One morning she had
been lured from the temple by the breeze
from the quayside. Lost in a dream of fish,
she had met a bearded stranger in the alley.
She had paused, one foot uplifted, waiting for
him to step aside. Instead, rough hands seized
her and thrust her into the sudden darkness of
a sack. Such outrage! Then such endless blind
jogging! Such sickness, such hunger, thirst
and the unbearable smell of her own filth!
Such useless gnawing and clawing to escape!

Finally, rough guttural voices and the
chink of coins.

'Sure she's good at killing rats?'

'Good? She's the reason there's always
corn in Egypt. Have you never seen the
Egyptians' granaries? How d'you think they
keep rats out? These creatures are such ratters
the Egyptians worship them.'

The other man made a noise of disgust,
deep in his throat.

'You are asking me to take a devil of

Gehenna into my house!'

'Better a devil than rats, brother. The price of this particular devil is still seven denarii. If the Egyptians had found her in my baggage they would have slain me.'

Her sack was rudely thrust into ruder hands. The neck was pulled open, and she was tipped on to a mud floor so hard it hurt her paws. Then a door slammed and she was in the dark again. She sat down and washed her shoulder to calm herself. Suddenly a rustling among the straw made her ears prick. At least she would not go hungry.

When she had killed and fed, she found a hole in the wall and rapidly enlarged it. Outside, in an utterly strange blurred landscape, and a thousand smells, all alien, she crouched to relieve herself. She was free; but all roads were the same, and none gave even a whiff of Bubastis, no matter how much she widened her nostrils to the breeze. From that day, her prison became her safe place and hunting ground. Her new owner, picking over the remains of her kills, was well pleased, and ignored her.

Others were less kind. When she descended to the ground men cursed and kicked her, and children threw stones; so she learned to keep to the rooftops and the night. But when the weight grew in her belly, and the flurry of kicking inside warned her that the time had come to find a safer place still, she knew she must not stay in that barn . . .

She had turned away from the stable door when an even crueller blast of wind caught

her, at the same time as the first contraction
in her belly. Making the bitterest of choices,
she turned again, and slipped inside. It was
dark, but to her eyes clear as crystal. Near
the door a plough-ox chewed the cud lazily,
lying half on its side. The straw where it lay
was thick and clean, but no good for a nest.
The creature might roll, crushing mother and
kitten altogether in the moment of birth . . .

Further in a grey donkey stamped. A
striped blanket had been thrown over its
back, and a man fussed around it with
furrowed brow and a cross, anxious voice.
His breath and the donkey's steamed together
in the frosty air. Further in still, a woman
lay, on straw not so thick and clean as the
ox's bed. A lamp gave her light, and enough
warmth to hold her hands out to. And there
was a patch of shadow in the corner behind.
The cat crept forward, silently, sagging belly
pressed close to the floor.

But the man saw her, shouted. Reached

for a long stick. He blocked her retreat. She leapt into the shadowed corner, back arched and teeth bared. The man advanced, but the woman put up her hand.

'Nay. Have mercy. She is in the same plight as myself. Are we so poor we can't share what we have?'

'Dirty things . . . if the child should be born tonight . . . they lie on children's faces and steal their breath . . .'

'Nay. She will soon have enough to keep her busy. And see, she is clean. She is the cleanest thing in this poor place.' The man turned, spreading his hands.

'I'm sorry! I *always* stay with my father's cousin when I come here. He must have known I was coming for the census. So why is his house full of strangers? I will tell you why. Because strangers have money. It is the Romans' fault; they destroy the old ways . . .'

'Husband, husband. Calm yourself. You are not to blame for your father's cousin. I

shall do well enough here.' The man grunted, soothed.

'But let the little cat stay. She will keep me company. All women find this waiting dreary. See, she's snuggling in.'

And, certainly, the cat's fear seemed quite gone. She crouched against the woman's robe, kneading furiously with her forepaws.

The cat could not understand it. She could feel the draughts catching at her fur, yet she was deliciously warm. The spiky straw seemed as soft as a silken temple cushion. And though the lamp guttered, the room seemed bathed in golden light, brighter than the sun on the temple of Bastet-Ra. She slowly crept up the robe, till her nose rested against the woman's neck. But the woman formed a nest in the straw of the dark corner, and put the cat into it; and there presently two kittens were born. Two only, for the winter-gods had been merciful. She purred with pleasure at having company during the

birth; in the temple at
such times, she-
cats were never
left alone . . .
Licked dry,
the kittens
began
to purr also;
tiny bee-like
buzzings.
And thus,
contented,
they must
all have
slept.

For when the she-cat wakened, there had
been a great change. Even the big animals, in
their stupidity, were aware of it, let alone a
god-cat. The lazy ox had lumbered to its feet
and was staring, drooling in shining strands
right down to its straw. The donkey had
stopped wheezing and stood quite still. Both

were intent on a feeding-trough in which lay a man-kitten.

But an even greater change had taken place. Glowing winged figures stood silent around. They were as tall as trees. Yet they all stood within the small stable. The cat, quite outfaced, sat up also, licked her shoulder to soothe her nerves. Then, greatly daring, she walked across to the first great figure and, one paw raised enquiringly, sniffed it. The scent of the creature was overpoweringly beautiful; better even than the lotus-flower in summer. She went on to the next, and the next. Each smelt differently, but all Heavenly.

Among the winged figures came a ripple of mirth.

'The cat sees us. Even the ox and ass. Why cannot the man?'

For the man was walking up and down, frowning thunderously.

'Are you sure you're all right? Is the child well? I would be happier if the midwife came

to look at you . . .' He walked straight through one of the great winged figures. The cat, watching, arched her back in alarm. But nothing happened, except another ripple of mirth among the winged creatures.

'Husband, we have no need of a midwife. It was an easy birth. How could it have been otherwise?'

The man grunted, deep in his throat. 'Oh, I know, I know.'

'Cannot you even feel those who guard us? The little cat can *see* them!'

Just then, the Child opened His eyes. The golden light that had been in the stable was as nothing to that which was suddenly there. The glowing beings covered their faces with their wings. But the she-cat inched towards him, as if drawn by a magnet.

'Look out, Mary, the cat!'

But the furry body stopped short, feet folded beneath her and green eyes blinking as she might have blinked at a fire. And such

121

a storm of purring as threatened to shake her apart. The woman said, 'Let her worship also.'

The cat dozed again, till the door banged back and the frosty wind blew in. Five men stood there, in greasy sheepskins. Their eyes seemed to fill their faces, and their mouths were permanently open. Having shut the door, they shuffled uneasily.

'This be un place. See, there's babe in feeding-trough. And more o' they bright-shining fellers. Beggin' yer pardon, gaffer.' They all bobbed to the nearest winged creature.

The woman's husband came forward.

'What are you jabbering about? You can't come in here. We're packed out already.'

'But the shining feller spoke to us. Told us we were to come, and what we'd find. And here it be, just like he said . . .'

And without another word, they knelt to the Child. The cat shifted uneasily but held

her station, even when the newborn lamb
bleated loudly, leapt from a shepherd's arms,
and ran straight into the oil lamp, nearly
setting the straw alight. Stupid creature,
thought the cat. But then lambs were not
reared in temples . . .

The shepherds left in the end, persuaded to
take their noisy lamb.

'It needs its mother,' said the woman.

The Child slept again, and the great light
dimmed, but did not depart. The man sat
in the doorway, as if on guard, but soon he
pulled his robe up around his ears, his head
dropped, and he slept the racking, snoring
sleep of exhaustion.

The woman closed her eyes, but did not
sleep. The smile stayed on her face, even
when she eased her aching body on the straw.
The cat lay, desiring never to move from this
place again.

But in the far corner, something rustled in
the straw. The cat's ears pricked. She turned.

A rat was coming towards the Child. It moved slowly on its belly, as if dazed. Its little red eyes shone.

Outrage filled the cat. The worst thing in her world was approaching the best. She wriggled her lean bottom and pounced. The rat squealed once as she bit into its neck. The man and woman came to, with a start.

Then they saw what had happened. 'See, she guards the Child,' said the woman sleepily.

'They have their uses,' grudged the man, and dozed again. The taste of rat's blood in her mouth made the cat feel ravenous.

But far more important, she now had a gift to bring the man–kitten. She crept nearer, dragging the limp body. The Child opened his blue eyes, and the cat laid the rat by Him.

But there was no praise or pleasure for her. The Child's grief over the rat broke over her like a storm, till she hunched her body, laid back her ears, and whimpered in pain.

The Child tossed restlessly, flung out one tiny arm towards the rat. The creature's poor death-flattened belly gave one frantic heave, its eyes opened and shone red and bright. Slowly it dragged itself to its feet and inspected itself with a bewildering twitching nose.

Then side-by-side, cat and rat watched, until the cock crowed.

By the time rich men came, the kittens had their ears half-pricked and their eyes wide open, and they were driving the she-cat frantic with their wobble-legged journeys through the straw. When the Child heard them draw near, He would give a gurgle of delight. The kittens were well fed, sleek like their mother. But not with the killing of rats, not ever. There was no need; now there were always scraps in plenty.

When the rich men had presented their gifts, and were sitting at ease with the mother, they noticed the cat.

'So the star has led others here before us?'

'How so?' asked the woman.

'Even the gods of Egypt come to worship. This is a sacred cat from Bubastis's temple on the Nile. When did they bring her? She is a gift greater than ours.'

'She arrived on her own, in the very hour of the Child's birth.'

'Incredible,' said Melchior.

'Unbelievable,' said Caspar.

'Egypt knows the stars,' said fierce-moustached Belthasar.

'What manner of god is this Bastet-Ra?' asked the woman, curious. 'Does she demand blood-sacrifice?'

'Nay,' said Melchior. 'She is a gentle god, a country-people's god. She brings fertile harvests. Maidens pray to her for a husband, and married women for an easy childbirth. Her worship is through dances and merriment and the right mothering of children. Egypt is a kindly place, under her rule.'

'She is a demon,' said Joseph. Recent events had mellowed him a little, but not much.

'Nay, husband, be not so narrow. Good is always good. These good men are not of our ways either, but they have come so far to be here. Tell me, Melchior, of the place this little one came from.'

So Melchior spoke of the broad-bosomed

Nile, and the yearly flood that brought fat crops, so that none starved. And the people going down the river to Bubastis, singing and dancing on the brown-winged ships.

'Poor little one,' said the woman, stroking the cat's fur. 'How you must miss the sun.'

The rich men had gone. They had talked of Herod; and when they talked of Herod, they lowered the lids of their shrewd eyes, and shook their heads. Something worried their subtle minds. When they left, they didn't go back to Jerusalem, though that would have been their easiest way.

There was always peace in the stable; but less than usual that night. The man tossed and groaned in his sleep. Suddenly, he awakened with a frightened shout.

'What ails you, husband?'

'I have seen an angel of the Lord.'

'Thanks be to God he has taken away your blindness.'

'You do not understand. It was the Dark

Angel: the Angel of Death.'

Clinging together, they turned to look at the sleeping Child.

'What are we to do? Were you not told?'

The man laughed harshly.

'I was told to do one thing, that I should have done days ago. I was told to take that devil back to its owner.' He threw a stick at the cat, which missed. The cat withdrew into a corner, calling the kittens to her urgently.

'But we do not know the owner . . .'

'*I* do – I have asked around. Aaron bar Joshua. A godless man who bought her from a Syrian camel driver . . .'

'But how will that help us?'

The man gave a laugh as short as a curse.

'The angel forgot to mention that.'

The woman said thoughtfully, 'Aaron bar Joshua is *not* the owner. He bought her from a thief. Her real owner dwells in the land of Egypt I . . .'

'Woman, we cannot go to Egypt. How

would we live? They are expecting us back at Nazareth. We have tarried *here* too long . . .'

'Would you disobey an angel, Joseph? Even *that* angel?'

In spite of the great danger, there was a last ripple of mirth among the great winged figures; their light was dimmer, now, but the cat could still sense them.

'We shall take this little one home,' said the woman, in a voice that was low but determined. 'And we shall make a home there ourselves, until another angel comes.'

★

And so, next morning, they packed hastily. And Joseph's father's cousin, repenting of his coldness (and having heard some talk of kings, gifts and a Messiah), found he could lend them all manner of things, including a second donkey. And so they went from Bethlehem more comfortably than they had come. And on the second donkey's back, twin kitten-heads poked from among the baggage.

And as each dawn turned the sky pink over the distant lands of Egypt, a swift long-legged streak ran before them, across the flat plains of Sinai.

The cat of Bastet-Ra was going home.

# Hysterical Herod and the Three Wise Men

## Anna Wilson

Herod was sitting on his throne. His left hand was receiving a massage from a beautiful concubine. His right hand was receiving a manicure from a delightful slave. His feet were in a bowl of warm, perfumed water – which was just as well, as they stank of ripe goat's cheese.

All was calm in the royal household.

'How I love the regal life,' the king

thought to himself. 'It's not even as if I have to rule that much. The Romans do that for me. So I get the girls, the gold and the gear for free! Oh lucky me . . .'

Unfortunately for Herod, God had other plans, and He'd decided to announce them this very morning.

'Ahem!' A slave was standing in the

doorway to the royal chamber, coughing discreetly in an attempt to get Herod's attention. 'Your Majesty has some visitors.'

Herod scowled irritably. He didn't like being interrupted when he was working so hard at doing nothing. 'Whadda they want?' he asked, in a most unkingly manner.

'If Your Majesty pleases,' grovelled the slave, 'they are three most distinguished and wise men from the East. They say they have come to worship a king, but if Your Majesty is indisposed—'

Herod cut in quickly, beaming through his beard. 'Oh, it's *worshipping* they want, is it? Well, what are you waiting for? Stop grovelling and bring them in right away! I'm never indisposed when someone wants to come to worship.'

Herod dismissed his slaves and concubine with a flick of his hands, which sent the nail files and hand creams flying in all directions. The king quickly shoved the mess under his

throne, put his shoes back on, patted his hair, adjusted his crown and smoothed down his beard.

'Ready!' Herod called excitedly. 'Er, I mean ENTER!'

The door to the royal chamber creaked open again and three tall, serious men glided into the room. Herod was rather put out to see that they all had much more impressive beards than he did, but then he remembered they'd come to worship him, so he sat back and prepared to be adored.

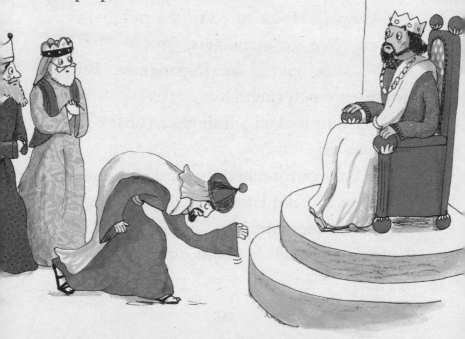

'Fire away!' he commanded.

The three wise men glanced at each other
with puzzled expressions on their faces.
Then one of them whispered: 'I think that's
Hebrew for "I'm listening" – tell him who
we are.'

The tallest king stepped forward and
bowed dramatically, sweeping his silken white
beard along the floor.

'I am Melchior, Your Majesty,' he
announced in a deep, sonorous voice. 'I
have come from the East with Balthazar
and Caspar.' He gestured to the other two
visitors. 'We are astrologers.'

'Yes, yes,' Herod said impatiently. 'Where
are my presents then?'

Melchior looked a little taken aback at this
and faltered.

So Balthazar stepped forward and bowing
as low as his fellow traveller, he explained:
'We study the stars, Your Majesty. The stars
have much to tell us about our lives on this

136

earth. In recent times, a new star has appeared in the heavens above our home country of Persia. It is a star announcing the birth of a new king. It was moving across the heavens, and so we have been following it. It has led us thus far to Your Majesty's most worthy city of Jerusalem, and so that is why we are here.'

Herod was not the brightest of kings, and this story had left him totally befuddled.

'A star? A new king? No, sorry – don't get it,' he said, shaking his head stubbornly.

Caspar now came forward, did the bowing and scraping thing and took his place next to the other two wise men.

'Your Majesty, where is the baby born to be the King of the Jews? We have come to worship him,' he said simply.

The poor wise men could not have been prepared for the effect these words would have on King Herod. First his already ruddy features turned a deep, dark crimson. Then he bared his teeth like a gruesome grizzly bear. Then steam shot out of his ears and his body seemed to lift a few feet from his throne as he bellowed:

'*I* AM THE KING OF THE JEWS, AND NO ONE CALLS *ME* A BABY!'

Melchior, Caspar and Balthazar stepped back in shock.

'W–With respect, Your Majesty, that is not what we meant,' Melchior stammered.

'We had hoped that Your Majesty would

tell us where the baby was,' Caspar explained.

'GET OUT!' Herod roared. 'GET OUT OF MY SIGHT!'

The three wise men did as they were told: they gathered up their beards and beat a hasty retreat.

Herod quivered with rage. 'SLAVE!' he shouted.

The slave who had shown in the visitors came running at once. 'Sire?' he asked, trembling. He'd seen Herod's ears steaming before, and he knew it was not a good sign.

'Get me my chief priests and the teachers of the Law NOW!' Herod commanded.

The slave hesitated. 'I can get the teachers of the Law, but the chief priests are slaughtering a goat right now so—'

'NOW!!!!' Herod roared. The room was so full of steam that Herod's beard had gone all frizzy. The slave summed up the seriousness of the situation and ran out.

In less time than it takes to tie your

Roman sandals, the slave was back with all the chief priests and the teachers of the Law in tow.

'Your Majesty requested our presence?' asked the first chief priest, bowing and trying to hide the bloodstains on his robe.

'I certainly did,' Herod said. 'I've just been told a baby's been born who's claiming to be the King of the Jews!' he shouted indignantly.

This announcement immediately got the teachers of the Law very excited. 'Now technically that is not possible, Your Majesty. You see babies can't *talk*, so—'

'Imbeciles!' Herod cried. 'I know that. Listen. You know all those things the prophets said yonks ago about a Messiah? Well, I think he's been born – today – near here! Our number's up!' And he proceeded to tell the teachers and the priests what the wise men had said.

'Calm yourself, Sire,' said the first chief priest. 'The prophets said, and I quote,

"Bethlehem in the land of Judah, you are by no means the least of the leading cities of Judah; for from you will come a leader who will guide my people of Israel."'

Herod stared at the priest and said, 'So?'

A teacher of the Law piped up: 'What he means is, Sire, that *technically*, the scriptures have led us to believe that the Messiah will be born in *Bethlehem*, not here in *Jerusalem*, so Your Majesty has nothing to worry about.'

'NOTHING TO WORRY ABOUT?' Herod's ears started steaming again. 'If a new king of the Jews has been born, it doesn't matter whether it's here, in Bethlehem or on the moon! It means that people will start worshipping him instead of me and that's NOT FAIR!' And, embarrassingly, he began to blub.

The chief priests and the teachers of the Law shifted uncomfortably from foot to foot and muttered among themselves.

'He's got a point, you know.'

'If the Messiah has come, there'll be no more jobs for the boys.'

'We need to hush this up before word gets out.'

Eventually, one of the teachers of the Law spoke up. 'Dry your eyes, Your Majesty. I'm sure we can get out of this one on a *technicality*. I advise that Your Majesty calls *back* the three wise men and asks them to find out *exactly* where this baby has been born. Say you want to go and worship him *too* or something. Then you can find him – and *kill* him.'

Herod stopped blubbing at once. He stared open-mouthed at the teacher of the Law. Then an evil glint lit up in his eyes. And a sly smirk spread across his face.

'BRILLIANT!' he cried.

And so that's what he did. He called Melchior and Balthazar and Caspar back. He asked them to find the baby so that he

could worship him too.

So the three wise men went on their way and followed the star to Bethlehem. And they did find the baby. And they did worship him – with presents of gold, frankincense and myrrh. And then they had a dream, in which God warned them not to go back to the murderous King Herod.

And the rest, as they say, is history . . .

# Holly and Ivy and Bah Humbug

## Karen McCombie

'**A**ndrea! There's a funny-looking dog rummaging in the bin bag outside!'

I frown in the direction of my dad, who has just yelled at my mum (Andrea) while I'm on the phone, about ten centimetres away from him. Annoyingly, my dad doesn't notice that a) I'm on the phone, or b) I'm frowning at him.

'What's the big deal?' I hear Mum calling

down from the spare room, where she's unpacking the Christmas decorations to put on the tree we're all going out to buy this Saturday morning. 'It'll be Mrs King's dog. She always lets it wander about on its own.'

'Nah – it's not Elvis!' Dad bellows back, acting like Mum is on another continent, instead of just on another floor of our house. 'This one's kind of scruffy-looking and white – you can hardly see it against the snow.'

'*Dad!* I'm on the *phone*!' I spell it out to him, but he just grins and mouths 'Bah Humbug!' at me and carries on stomping up the stairs so he can yak on to Mum about some unimportant dog minding its own business and chewing on a bin bag or whatever.

But anyway, Dad's not the only one who's bugging me while I'm trying to have a conversation.

'Lemme speak to her! Can I speak to Auntie Judy? Please, *please*, Holly?'

That's my little sister, Ivy. Just like always, she isn't waiting for me to answer her – she's just trying to grab the phone while I'm still talking. All I can do to stop her (without resorting to thumping her, which I'm *very* tempted to do sometimes, no matter how cute and adorable Mum and Dad think she is) is to keep swivelling around so she can't reach the receiver.

'Hey, Holly, have you thought of a present you'd like yet?' says the voice in my ear, unaware that I'm struggling to carry on this chat uninterrupted. 'You know how

146

I like to get some hints, so I don't get you something you'll hate!'

The voice in my ear belongs to my Auntie Judy. She's calling from the Isle of Mull, which is in Scotland. (Actually, being an island, it's not so much *in* Scotland as floating alongside it.) I don't get to see Auntie Judy too often, since she lives a very *looooonnnnnngggg* train journey, a very bumpy ferry crossing and a car ride away from us, but I really like her. Except at this time of year, when she says insensitive stuff like, 'Have you thought of a present you'd like yet, Holly?'

The problem I have is with the word 'present'. I don't want a 'present'; I want 'presents' – two to be exact. Don't go thinking I'm being horrible and greedy; it's just that it's not fair, having your birthday two days after Christmas. Everyone – including Auntie Judy and my grandparents and my mum and dad – has this INFURIATING habit of buying me a 'joint'

present to cover Christmas *and* my birthday. Or buying me a 'big' gift for Christmas, and then getting me just 'little', 'fun' and 'extra' prezzies for my birthday. But it's not fair, is it? My best mate, Saskia, doesn't get a 'big' present at Christmas and then just some bath bombs and a new pencil case for her birthday in June, does she? But that's what happens to me, just 'cause I have the bad luck to be born on the twenty-seventh of December.

'Well, I s'pose I would kind of like—'

Maybe I'm sounding a bit half-hearted when I try to answer Auntie Judy's question (not surprisingly), but I wouldn't mind getting the chance to *finish* the sentence. Unfortunately, Ivy has other ideas, and bounces like a hyperactive Tigger all around me, finally snatching the phone from my hand before I manage to blurt out to Auntie Judy that I'm pretty keen on this how-to-paint-stained-glass kit I saw in our local art shop.

'Auntie Judy! It's *me*! It's Ivy!' my sister gabbles, keeping up the bouncing routine, like she's most definitely Tigger and not a six-just-about-to-go-on-seven-year-old girl.

She's bouncing 'cause she thinks it's cute and adorable, and that I'll be so overwhelmed by how cute and adorable she is (ha!) that I won't make a fuss and try to yank the phone back from her. But the thing is, I can't be bothered. I know I sound horribly grumpy, but for eleven and a half months out of twelve I really am a bright and happy person (except when Ivy is winding me up, of course). It's just that this whole Christmas/birthday thing gets me ratty, and it doesn't help that Dad's nicknamed me 'Bah Humbug' – after some Christmas-hating party-pooper in this ancient story he's into – just 'cause he can't see I've gone a bit ratty.

And if some dumb nickname isn't bad enough, there's also the fact that I get teased something rotten about my stupid *real* name at this particular time of the year . . .

Oh yes. Since I'm in a moaning mood (sorry), let me moan a bit about being called Holly. I got named 'Holly' because I was born at Christmas time. Maybe that sounds sort of cute and OK, if only my sister hadn't been born exactly *three years and one day* after me, and Mum and Dad hadn't decided to get all inspired by the festive season again and call her Ivy. So we're Holly and Ivy, just like the Christmas carol. It's so wet and corny, as the kids in my class just LOVE to remind me when Christmas rolls round.

'Ha ha ha!' Darren Sharp laughed at me yesterday. 'Why didn't your parents call you and your sister "Santa" and "Claus"? Or "Snow" and "Flake"?'

'Yeah? And why didn't yours just call you "Dork"?' I suggested to him, feeling my face flush holly-berry red with rage.

Still, only my name and birthday are to

blame for irritating me at Christmas. The one thing that can irritate me the whole year round is bouncing around the hall about a metre away from me. Why, why, *why* did I end up with someone as annoying as Ivy for a sister? You're going to think I'm being mean and grouchy again, but seriously, all me and my sister have got in common is a) the same parents, b) lousy festive names, and c) the fact that our birthdays are so close to Christmas. Otherwise, we can't stand each other. The TV programmes *I* like, she yawns at. The pop stars *she* likes, I think are more dorky than Darren Sharp. Every time I try to talk to Mum and Dad, she bounces, bounds and yabbers away, so they get all starry-eyed and charmed and pay attention to her instead of me. Every time she tries to talk to Mum and Dad, I can't help yawning, 'cause whatever she yabbers on about is so dull and stupid I need coat hangers hooked under my eyelids to keep me from falling asleep.

'Um . . . I dunno,' I hear Ivy say to Auntie Judy, finally quitting her hyperactive bounding and letting her bare feet rest on the spot on the carpet.

Whether Ivy still half expects me to grab the phone back or not, I don't care – I've lost interest, and find myself wandering over to the kitchen windowsill and staring out.

At a dog, as it happens.

And Dad is right – it's *not* Mrs King's Elvis. Elvis is fat and shiny and black-furred, but this dog is different. Its fur is white and dull and goes in all directions, as if it's been brushed by a madman, or not brushed for weeks. Narrowing my eyes, I decide that it can't have been brushed – or fed – for a long time, from the scruffy way it looks and the frantic licking going on with that empty tuna tin it's dragging from the bin bag.

'What are you looking at?' Ivy's irritating voice pipes up right beside me. Has she finished her conversation with Auntie Judy

already? It was hardly worth her making such a fuss about grabbing the phone from me in the first place.

'A dog,' I tell her flatly, keeping my eyes fixed on the snuffling stray outside. And I'm sure it *is* a stray – it couldn't look less loved if it was dumped in a bin bag itself.

'Awww! It's cute!'

It's not often Ivy says something I agree with (usually when she speaks she comes out with something so loud and irritating that I wish I carried earplugs around with me). But she's right – it *is* a cute dog. It's staring up at us right now with the soppiest honey-brown eyes I've ever seen, all guilty and sad and lonely at the same time.

'Let's go out and pat it,' Ivy announces, ready to haul the back door open and bounce outside, even if her feet are bare and there's a whole heap of snow on the path.

'Hold it! Not so loud. It's nervous and you'll scare it away,' I tell her. 'Go and put your shoes on while I get something for it to eat.'

For a few seconds we both silently bustle about, Ivy pulling on her new winter boots, and me rifling through the fridge and finding some smoked turkey that Dad likes for his sandwiches.

'It's still there, Holly,' Ivy mumbles, standing on tiptoes in her red suede boots and squashing her nose on the glass panel of the back door. 'Can we go and pat it now?'

But 'cause *I'm* the big sister, I decide to be the one to reach across and slowly turn the door handle. It squeaks really badly and I don't trust Ivy not to yank it and squeak it so

loudly that our scrawny visitor sprints off in alarm, sending the tuna tin spinning.

'Hello, baby,' Ivy coos, wriggling through the gap practically before I've even got the door open.

I peer out, half expecting the dog to be backing away, but it's still hovering nervously by our overflowing bin.

'It's shivering!' Ivy says sorrowfully, and before I can tell her to be careful and go slowly in case it bites, she bounds over and wraps her arms around the neck of the startled dog.

OK, so it hasn't bitten her – that's a good start. But from the look of its manky fur, Ivy *might* end up with a few bites . . . of the *flea* variety.

'Hey doggy, want this?'

The dog flinches a little, as if it's more used to getting a smack from a hand coming its way than the offer of some food. But one cautious sniff and it realizes its mistake and delicately snatches the cold meat from my hand, like it's worried I might change my mind and whisk it away.

'You're hungry, aren't you, doggy?' Ivy whispers, nudging its head with her nose (and probably picking up a few germs while she's at it). 'It's a stray, isn't it, Hol? It's hungry and dirty and it doesn't have a collar.'

'Maybe.' I shrug vaguely, but I'm thinking exactly the same thing. 'Hey, Ivy, let it go and let's see if I can get it to come over to the back door . . .'

Reluctantly, Ivy loosens her grip as I walk backwards, holding out another turkey slice as bait. It's then that I spot a funny red mark on Ivy's skinny wrist, poking out from the sleeve of her lilac jersey.

'What's that? On your arm?' I ask her, flipping my eyes from the red mark to the timidly following dog.

'Chinese burn,' Ivy shrugs, taking baby steps alongside the dog and patting it reassuringly as it makes its wary way towards me and the back door.

'How come you got that?' I ask her, as another turkey slice gets gulped in one go.

'Got in a fight with Harry in my class,' she explains.

'What about?'

I don't know Harry, or anyone else in Ivy's class apart from her best friend, Melina, who comes around for regular squealing and bouncing sessions at ours. But suddenly I really, *really* don't like this boy I've never heard of.

'We did letters for Santa at school yesterday. No one was supposed to look, but Harry read what I'd asked for and told me I was stupid. I told him I wasn't, and he hit me. So I thumped him back and then he gave me a Chinese burn. Then the teacher saw and told us both off for fighting.'

'But that's not fair!' I frown, as the white dog takes another few paw pads through the snow and swallows another turkey slice.

'I know,' Ivy shrugs again, sounding very grown-up and matter-of-fact about the whole incident. 'Hey, look – it's nearly there! Give it some more turkey, Holly!'

'Yeah, yeah, OK, Ivy,' I tell her, stepping up on to the doorstep and pulling another piece of meat from the plastic packet. 'But what did that horrible kid think was so stupid about your Santa letter? What did you ask for?'

'A new birthday. And a new name.'

Um . . . I guess I'd expected her to say a complete collection of *Pop Idol* videos, or a trampoline for extra bouncing, or some kind of doll's house for her stupid dolls, or something. I hadn't expected her to

want . . . well, what *I* wanted.

'But how come?' I ask her, looking at my kid sister in wonder.

'Well, I want a new birthday 'cause mine is too close to Christmas and no one ever gives me two proper presents. Even Auntie Judy asked me what I wanted as a joint present just now on the phone,' says Ivy, twining her fingers into the white dog's fur. 'And Ivy's a *stupid* name. Specially when I've got a sister called Holly. Harry and the other boys have been teasing me about it ever since we've been practising Christmas carols for the school concert.'

Wow!

Wow that my sister has the same grudge against our birthdays and our names. I thought she hadn't noticed. I thought Ivy was always too busy bouncing and charming the pants off everyone to care about stuff like that.

And wow that I've been so surprised by

what Ivy has just said that I hadn't noticed
that we've got all the way into the kitchen —
me, Ivy and the white dog. Ivy is quietly
closing the door and the dog is gazing
around, sniffing the air for lingering Saturday
morning breakfast smells. It still seems
nervous, but — and I'm not exactly an expert
on dogs — it looks kind of, well, *happy* to me.

'Holly? Ivy? Are you two nearly ready?' We
hear Dad's voice call out, as his footsteps begin
thumping downstairs. 'Let's get shopping for
that tree — and see if we can't find you two a
great present each while we're at it!'

At the sound of Dad's cheery but gruff
tone, the dog's honey-brown eyes flicker
worriedly from my face to Ivy's, with one
ear tilted up and the other flopping down
pathetically.

'Don't worry. It's all right,' I tell the dog,
reaching out and ruffling the floppy ear.

'Holly!' Ivy hisses at me urgently, as Dad's
footsteps thump down the last few stairs. 'I

don't care about present shopping! Can't we ask to keep the dog? Like a special Christmas and birthday present all rolled into one – for both of us?'

The dog gazes up at me pleadingly, same as Ivy does.

But neither of them need to plead. For only the second time ever, I totally agree with my annoying little sister. I don't care about a new pair of trainers or a CD player or a stained glass art set. I want this scruffy white dog. And I know it won't be easy – first we'll have to convince Mum and Dad that it's a great idea, then we'll have to do the right thing and check with the police that no one has reported a missing white dog (and I bet six mince pies and a Christmas pudding that no one *will* have, the state it's in).

'It's a deal!' I smile at Ivy and the dog.

Ivy seems about to smile back, when she catches sight of our dad, standing stock still in the kitchen doorway.

Immediately she goes into full bouncy, cute, adorable mode, and for once it doesn't bug me.

'Look, Dad!' Ivy trills, jumping up and doing her best Tigger impersonation, startling the white dog while she's at it. 'It's a puppy! Do you think it's for us? Or is it an early birthday prezzie from you and Mum, for me and Holly?' *I'm* the big sister, but suddenly Ivy's in charge, and when she zaps me a quick sideways glance to help her out, I do my best.

'It's really friendly, Dad,' I chip in, throwing an arm around the dog (it's definitely a grown-up dog and *not* a puppy). 'And we've thought of a name for it already – it's called . . . it's called . . . Bah Humbug! Humbug for short!'

The scruffy white dog pants happily, as though living here and being called Humbug is the best news it's heard in a *long* time. Or maybe it's just panting at the last slice of turkey it's spotted me holding in my other hand.

'Er, Andrea . . .' Dad shouts over his shoulder, a grin a mile wide spreading across his face. 'There's a funny-looking dog in our kitchen now!'

'*What?!*' we hear Mum squawk from upstairs.

But squawks or not, that grin of Dad's tells me and Ivy and Bah Humbug that this *might* just be the *best* Christmas/birthday present any of us has ever had.

Though maybe we'll need to ask Santa to bring us a can of flea spray . . .

# Loving and Giving

Rumer Godden

'Christmas is a time for giving as well as getting.' Every child knows that; even two- or three-year-olds are initiated into secret buyings and wrapping ups; all autumn, children spend hours in making things, those heavy-as-lead carpentry gifts (Mother and Father paying for wood), raffia mats, cross-stitch kettle-holders, embroidery, home-bound books. 'You must not only give, you

must love to give,' our mother insisted, and
in spite of the work it was easy to love this
planning and spending; but when it came
to giving away our *own* presents, presents
we had been given, it was quite another
idea and in our Indian childhood it seemed
exceedingly hard that we, four sisters, were
never allowed to keep a single thing from any
of the Christmas 'dollies'.

A 'dolly' – I must explain – was not a doll;
it was the name given to the baskets of gifts
brought on Christmas morning by Indian
merchants, contractors and head members
of the office staffs as compliments to their
Christian clients and employers.

It had become a custom, and custom had
built up a ritual for it. The dollies were not
handed over in the offices; they were
presents and had to be presented with Indian
courtesy which meant that every giver had
to call personally at each house and make
his salaams.

For the merchants and babus it must have been an arduous and expensive morning – for us it was a training in patience and obedience. My father and mother received on the front verandah; Mahommed Shah, our Big Mahommedan butler, regulated the queue, announcing each visitor in turn. Perhaps it would be one of my father's own babus resplendent in snow-white muslin shirt and dhoti – the long flowing cloth worn draped as a nether garment – coloured socks and sock suspenders, patent leather pumps; perhaps it was a Marwari, one of the merchants or stockbrokers, usually rich and dressed in a cream silk achkan – a long tunic coat – marigold-coloured turban, a fresh scarlet tika mark on his forehead. A tika mark is the small red spot painted between the eyebrows, put on by the priest after ritual bathing. Sometimes a Marwari would bring his children; they were in European clothes except for round velvet hats like pillbox lids

embroidered in gold. They had gold earrings too, and smelt strongly of coconut oil. At once an unspoken bond would spring up between us and them – the dolly things were not for them either.

The ritual was always the same: my father was garlanded, sometimes my mother; in a minute or so the long necklaces of jessamine or marigold flowers would be taken off and coiled on a tray held by Abdul, our officious nursery servant – Abdul had always to be in on every-thing – and as the morning went on the pyramid of garlands grew into a scented mountain. The caller was seated and five minutes would be spent in polite conversation. We children were not often brought into the foreground or the

conversation – my father and mother had no son and the calamity of four daughters, all of whom would presumably have to be dowried, was better ignored – but there was plenty to interest us; during the talk, the baskets were carried in by the caller's servants and put at my father's feet.

Dollies were always in light round baskets, of the sort coolies use, but now decorated with flowers and sheets of coloured paper. Sometimes there was only one, sometimes two or three, their number and cost depending on the richness of the giver, and the importance of my father's patronage to him; sometimes it was in genuine gratitude for help in the past year, but the giver knew, as my father knew – as everyone in India knew – that there was a code of strict limitation on the cost.

In the old East India Company days dollies were often bribes – and fabulous bribes. This suspicion of bribery still hung over them

and anything gold or silver, even children's
bangles, was immediately handed back; there
could be none of the exquisite gauze and
gold thread saris or scarves that came from
Benares; a bottle of whisky or a length of
plain silk was the utmost limit. Usually they
were only flowers, fruit, cakes, sweets and, for
us children, crackers and toys.

In spite of the semi-royal state in which
the English in India lived, we were brought
up quite frugally, not too much of anything,
certainly not many toys and we yearned after
these dollies. Certainly, I have never seen
anything more attractive: the foundation
was always fruit; red apples from Kulu,
bananas – sometimes a whole stem of them
was carried in and set beside the basket as
an extra – papayas, pomelos like big pink-
fleshed grapefruit, tangerines in silver paper,
nuts. To one side would be a Christmas cake,
florid with shop icing, which we thought
wonderful – our cake was homemade. There

would be a box of chocolates tied with ribbon – sometimes four boxes of chocolates for four sisters, never to be allowed to keep them. There were Indian sweets, jillipes, clear spiral rings of toffee sugar – or sandesh, which was a sort of fudge stuck with silver paper. Crackers and toys were poised on top. We duly had to thank for them; the caller airily waved his hand and said, 'They are nothing, nothing,' though they must have cost him many rupees. He then made way for the next visitor and the baskets were spirited away.

Not entirely spirited. They were taken to the dining-room, which in our Indian-built home was as large as a ballroom; there Nan, our Eurasian nurse, and our Ayah, unpacked them and arranged them on the dining-room table in pyramids of fruit, platters of sweets, rows of cakes, piles of crackers; the toys were heaped on the floor. As soon as the last caller had gone from the front verandah, the last car or tikka gharri – little box-like

carriages drawn by two ponies – driven away,
a familiar shuffling, rustling, whispering,
giggling and sniffling began on the back
verandah. The noise grew louder until
Mahommed Shah threw open the door and
in came the droves of the servants' children.

We were not rich people but we must
have had something like eighteen servants
then, Christian, Mahommedan, Hindus
of all castes, and there were between sixty
and eighty children including the dhobi's
(washerman's) clan, now mysteriously swelled
to double size – but my mother never sent
any of the little gatecrashers away. Some we
knew well as they lived in the compound;
some, like Mahommed Shah's, who had a
house nearly as large as ours, came only at
Christmas. Some were our enemies – there
had been scuffles and ambushes – some
our dear friends, but now one would have
thought we had never met before; we of the
back verandah were quite as ceremonious as

our elders of the front. There were, of course, no garlands but the children gave us salaams which we gravely returned.

The protocol was strict: Mahommed Shah's big girl and small boys stood near the table – they in clean shirts and dhotis, she in a Punjabi, the loose tunic and trousers, with a little gauze head or breast scarf worn by Mahommedan girls. All the gardeners' children stood apart; they were Brahmins, the priestly caste, the small girls were exquisite in saris, jessamine flowers in their hair. The dhobi's children were everywhere, some of them dressed only in a charm string and short cotton jacket that left their rice-swollen stomachs and private parts bare; the babies wore nothing at all except charm strings, but they were oiled all over. Far over by the door stood the sweeper's son and behind him a smaller boy who, unlike other children, was employed. He had the curious task – for which, touchingly, he would put on his only

shirt – of being fetched in to pick up and carry away the bodies of any dead crows that fell into the garden or any casualties among our guinea pigs. No other servant would or could touch a corpse, not even of a pet.

This protocol was not of our seeking; we were often companions of the sweeper's boy – he could fly our kites from the roof better than any of us – but we knew that now, as an untouchable, he must keep apart, just as we knew that the gardeners' children must not be given fruit or cakes or sweets; they would not be allowed to eat them because non-Brahminee hands had touched them, non-Brahminee shadows fallen on them, not only non-Brahminee; by Hindu ruling we, as western children, were untouchables as well. It was all part of the intricate web of rules and taboos that govern the whole of Indian social life: children could usually break through it, but not today. This was a public occasion.

'Can't we keep that *darling* little doll? One

little basket of cooking pots? One box of
chocolates?' But we never could. The answer
was always the same and it was the four of us
who were required to do the actual giving,
acting as reluctant little Lady Bountifuls. My
youngest sister Rose was a greedy child and
Nan sometimes had literally to prise a drum
of Turkish delight or a box of chocolates out
of her hand.

We parted with fruit and nuts; these
were tied swiftly into the corners of saris or
dhotis or collected by the dhobi's wife into
an old pillowcase. (The dhobi's wife always
fascinated us because she had elephantiasis.
We stared at her gargantuan feet and
ankles.) Then each of the children was given
an empty cracker box or its lid to hold.
These were filled with sweets; the boxes of
chocolates were ripped open or given whole
to a family. Then the Christmas cakes were
allotted and this was done in the unfair way
of the world – the largest and best cakes to

the richest children, the worst to the neediest, but my mother always kept a collection of inconspicuous pink iced cakes to help fill the maws of the small dhobis. At last came the moment for which everyone was really waiting – the distribution of the toys.

Why was it such a pang to part with these? Why did we like them so much? I suppose because no one else ever gave such things to us. We each had a sensible gift from our father and mother, probably something we had wanted all the year; in the evening we should each get something from the Club Christmas tree, but in this isolated place the dollies brought the only toys we saw from outside the great world, as it were. Some were Indian; miniature brass cooking pots, platters and ladles, or

wooden animals, miniature
too and painted with spots and
red daisies which made them
look seductive and all packed in
small chip baskets; there were
glass bangles
in jewel
colours which we were
not allowed to wear; wonderfully
cut paper balls; clay
gods and
goddesses;
and with
these were
western toys,
one for each
of us: cheap
clockwork
cars and trains,
wooden animals that
clacked and bounced,
celluloid toys, dolls with

fixed eyes, gummed-on clothes, chip
straw hats. Here again, the rich
had the best: Mahommed Shah's
daughter the most splendiferous
doll – the dhobi's the collection of
celluloids, but immediately after
came the crackers as consolation.
Crackers were always divided equally.

People say crackers are expensive
nonsense. I wish they could have seen those
children with them. 'A-aah! A-aah! Aie!
Aie!' Murmurs broke out all over the room.
The big kohl-darkened eyes grew bigger,
brown faces broke into smiles; the small
brown hands holding the cardboard box trays
trembled. Those crackers would be kept long
after the things inside had been taken out;
the gaudy fringed papers, the least tinselled
star be made a treasure. We liked giving the
crackers – by then we had been won over
and nothing mattered except that the children
should be made as contented as possible; but

then the ritual was finished. In a few minutes
the last child had salaamed and scurried away;
the baskets were picked up empty. Once
again everything was gone.

'Look where those children live, and look
where you . . .' Nan would scold. We knew
quite well where they lived, mostly in a line
of brick-built rooms behind the cookhouse,
one room to a family, one tap to a whole row.
The dhobi children lived in the wash court,
the grooms in a wicker hut beside the stable,
but we did not see anything wrong with this.
Indeed, it seemed gloriously simple; no nursery
or schoolroom, no coming down to the dining
room for meals, no changing to go into the
drawing-room, so few clothes; and to us those
little rooms were homelike, with their swept
earth floors, clay oven, shelf of brass cooking
pots, perhaps a day bed, the straw sleeping mats
rolled up, the family possessions in a tin trunk
painted with roses, the family umbrella hanging
from the rafters. The poorer the house, the

prettier, because it did not have such ugliness
as aluminium saucepans, army blankets, china
plates, petrol lamps. The children ate off banana
leaves with their fingers. At night the soft
flicker of a wick floating in an earthenware
lamp turned all the walls to gold. 'You are
so lucky,' Nan always said. They were lucky
too. 'And I don't see,' Rose said obstinately,
'why they should have our toys.'

'You wouldn't want to keep all those.'

'I would.' Rose was firm. She was young
enough to say what she thought unabashed,
but we could only feel; the fact that we knew
we were selfish only made it worse.

'You must not only give, you must love
giving.' Perhaps that early training grew
into our bones. I do love to give, yet still,
somewhere, at the back of my mind is an
unsatisfied yearning and I wish that somehow,
something that can never happen in far-off
England would happen, and I could have one
dolly entirely to myself.

# A Happy Christmas
# for the Ghost

## Martin Waddell

It was Christmas Eve, and the Ghost was busy decorating the coal shed. He had strung red and yellow streamers round the walls, and poked holly through the holes in the tin roof. A piece of mistletoe dangled in the doorway and the Ghost's picture of Florence Nightingale was draped in silver tinsel. In the far corner there glowed a ghostly Christmas tree, all red and green and gold and shiny.

'Oooooooooh!
Ghost!' said Bertie,
looking at it with
saucer eyes. He
thought it was the
best Christmas tree
he had ever seen.

The Ghost
sat down rather
unsteadily on the
slack, resting his
glass on the coal
bucket beside him.
The Ghost had just come
back from the Spectre's Arms, where he had
been having a small extra Festive Haunt, with
breaks for refreshments.

'It is time you were in bed, Bertie,' said
the Ghost. 'Santa Claus will soon be here.'

'Max says there is no Santa Claus,' said
Bertie.

'Max says there are no ghosts,' said the

Ghost. 'But Max doesn't know everything, does he? Ghosts are rather like Santa Claus.'

'Are they?' asked Bertie.

'Oh yes, they are,' said the Ghost. 'I'm a ghost, and you believe in me, so you can see me. Max *doesn't* believe in me, and he can't see me. It is the same with Santa Claus, but more important, because if nobody believed in Santa Claus, there would be no Christmas. I feel sorry for Max.'

'So do I,' said Bertie, and he went off upstairs to bed.

'Mum,' said Bertie, as Mrs Boggin was tucking him in. 'Mum, I'm sorry for Max, because Max doesn't believe in Santa Claus.'

'Doesn't he?' said Mrs Boggin.

'Mum,' said Bertie. 'Do *you* believe in Santa Claus?'

'Of course I do, wee Bertie,' said Mrs Boggin. 'You wait until the morning, and you'll see.'

'But you don't believe in ghosts, do you?'

said Bertie. 'You don't believe in *my* Ghost.'

Mrs Boggin took a long time replying. 'I don't know, Bertie,' she said, in the end. 'I don't know what to think about your Ghost. Sometimes I . . . but it doesn't really matter what I believe, does it? So long as *you* believe in him.'

'That's right,' said Bertie. 'My Ghost will still be there, as long as I believe in him.' And he cuddled down beneath the sheets to go to sleep.

But he didn't go to sleep.

Bertie lay in bed hoping and hoping for a red and yellow bike like the one in Mrs Boggin's big catalogue.

'Bikes cost a lot of money, Bertie,' Mrs Boggin had told him. 'But we'll see at Christmas time.'

Now it was Christmas, almost.

'Bike.'

'Bike.'

Bertie concentrated very hard in the hope

that believing in bikes would make one come.

The Ghost came floating into the room and perched on the end of Bertie's bed. He waved at Bertie.

'Just doing my rounds,' he said. 'I've got to make sure all the stockings are up.'

'Mine is one of Dad's,' said Bertie, who had picked the biggest sock he could find. Then he asked the Ghost a question.

'Ghost,' Bertie said, 'if Max doesn't believe in Santa Claus, what will happen to *his* Christmas stocking? You said there would be no Christmas if people didn't believe in Santa Claus, and Max doesn't.'

The Ghost looked serious. 'Then you'll have to do his believing for him, Bertie,' he said.

'Oh,' said Bertie. 'Do you think I could?'

'I'm sure you could,' said the Ghost.

'I believe in Santa Claus,' said Bertie.

'Oh, I know you do,' said the Ghost.

'Goodnight, Bertie,' and he glided off in the general direction of the Spectre's Arms and the Haunted Cellar Disco, where his presence was urgently required.

'Bike,' thought Bertie, thinking very hard, and 'I believe in Santa Claus for me *and* Max,' and 'BIKE,' again, and again, and again, because the bike was very important.

'BIKE!!!'

He went to sleep.

'Hip-yip hurrah! It's Christmas!' Max was dancing on the stairs. In one hand he waved a telescope, and in the other his half-empty Christmas stocking. He was eating mandarin oranges and chocolate at the same time, with a spud gun sticking out of the belt of his pyjamas.

Elsie said, 'Oooooh!' and 'Aaaaah!' and started eating too, while she sorted out the lovely things in her stocking. There was a blue scarf and a diary and a pen and a talking doll.

'Toooole-uuuu! Ouuutle-ooo!' went Bertie, on the gold trumpet he had pulled from his stocking. 'Tooole-utttle-utttttle!'

'Children, it is only six o'clock,' muttered a bleary-eyed Mr Boggin.

'Hip-yip! Ooooooo-aaah! Toootle-uuttttle-uttle!' went all the Boggins in chorus, as they headed down the stairs.

The door of the Christmas Room was shut.

The ghost bounced up and down in the hallstand, wearing his haunting hat and his pyjamas and eating chocolate doubloons from his stocking. 'Wait till you *see*! Wait till you *see* what's in there, Bertie!' he whispered.

'Now,' said Mrs Boggin, opening the door of the Christmas Room. 'One child at a time. Bertie first, because he is the smallest.'

Bertie went into the Christmas Room.

The curtains were pulled tight, the pile of presents was lit by the glint of the Christmas tree lights.

There were fat parcels and thin parcels, big parcels and little parcels and tiny parcels, and green parcels, and red parcels and gold parcels and yellow parcels, and parcels that looked like bottles and parcels that didn't, and a thing like a swing ball for Max and a huge painting set for Elsie (complete with easel) and . . .

. . . glittering in the darkness . . .

. . . red and yellow, with a shiny bright bell . . .

'Bike,' breathed Bertie. 'My BIKE!'

He touched it.

He rang the bell.

It was *real*.

It *really* was.

Everyone had a very happy Christmas at Number 12 Livermore Street.

'You only got that telescope from Santa

Claus because of me,' Bertie told Max, and Max didn't even thump him.

'You've all eaten too much!' said Mrs Boggin.

'Good,' said Mr Boggin, and the rest of the Boggins agreed with him. All except Tojo, that is, for he was still too busily engaged in chewing the biggest-rubber-bone-in-the-world (given to him by Max, and tied up with a blue ribbon by Elsie) to agree with anything.

'Time for bed,' said Mrs Boggin, at last.

They went to bed.

'Mum,' said Bertie, as she was tucking him in, 'the Ghost said I was to thank you very much for having him.'

'You can tell him it's a pleasure, Bertie,' said Mrs Boggin. And then she added, 'If I see him, I'll tell him myself.'

'You can't see him, Mum,' said Bertie. 'You can't see the Ghost if you don't believe in him.'

'Y-e-s,' said Mrs Boggin. 'Well . . . you see . . . Bertie, I think I—'

'Mum,' said Max, 'I think I've got a sick tummy.'

Mrs Boggin went to deal with Max's tummy. Then she had to rush downstairs to fetch Bertie's book about spiders, which Aunt Amanda had sent him from Ballynahinch. Elsie couldn't sleep, and wanted to get up and watch the late film. Then Mr Boggin couldn't find his slippers.

Mrs Boggin was run off her feet looking after them all.

'Bed,' said Mr Boggin, who had had a very hard day sitting down.

Mrs Boggin let Tojo out and in again, stoked up the boiler, put out the kitchen light, stole a nip of cold ham and turkey, and went into the Christmas Room. And there . . .

. . . shimmering in the glow of the Christmas lights . . .

. . . fast asleep in the best armchair with a large glass of Mr Boggin's Bristol Cream sherry in his hand . . .

. . . Mrs Boggin *saw* the Ghost.

She stood absolutely still, and her mouth dropped open.

'Bertie's Ghost!' she gasped.

'Is that you, Florence?' muttered the Ghost, still deep in sleep.

He didn't wake up and Mrs Boggins didn't wake him. Instead, she put out the light and tiptoed gently out of the room.

# Cobweb Christmas

### Shirley Climo

Once upon a Christmastime, long ago in
Germany, there lived a little old woman.
She was so little she had to climb upon a step
stool to reach her feather bed and so old she
couldn't even count all the Christmases she'd
seen. The children in her village called her
Tante, which means 'Auntie' in German.

Tante's home was a cottage at the edge
of a thick fir forest. The cottage had but one

room, one door and one window, and no
upstairs to it at all. It suited the old woman,
for there was room enough within its walls
for her to keep a canary for singing, a cat for
purring, and a dog to doze beside the fire.

Squeezed up against the cottage was a
barn. The barn was a bit bigger, and in it
Tante kept a donkey for riding, and a cow
and a goat for milk and cheese. She had a
noisy rooster as well to crow her out of bed
each morning, and a speckled hen to lay an
egg for her breakfast. With so many animals
about, the tiny cottage wasn't tidy, but Tante
didn't fuss over a few feathers, a little fur, or a
spider web or two.

Except once a year, when the days got
short and the nights grew long the old
woman would nod her head and say, 'Time
to clean for Christmas.'

Then she'd shake the quilt and wash the
window and scour the soot from the kettle.
She'd scrub the floor on her hands and knees

and stand tiptoe on her step stool to sweep
the cobwebs from the ceiling.

This Christmas was just as always.

'Wake up!' said Tante, snapping her fingers.
The dog stopped dreaming and dashed off to
dig for bones beneath the bushes.

'Scat!' cried Tante, flapping her apron. The

cat hid under the bedclothes and the canary flew to the chimney top.

'Shoo!' scolded Tante, swishing her broom. All the spiders and each little wisp of web went flying out the door as well.

When she'd washed and wiped every crack and corner of the cottage, the old woman nodded her head and said, 'Time to fetch Christmas.'

Then Tante took the axe from its peg in the barn and hung the harness with bells upon the donkey. She scrambled on to the donkey's back, nimble as a mouse, and the two jogged and jingled into the fir forest. They circled all around, looking for a tree to fit Tante's liking.

'Too big!' said she of some, and 'Crooked as a pretzel!' of others.

At last she spied a fir that grew straight, but not tall, bushy, but not wide. When the wind blew, the tree bent and bobbed a curtsey to the little old woman.

'It wants to come for Christmas,' Tante told the donkey, 'and so it shall.'

She chopped down the tree with her axe, taking care to leave a bough or two so it might grow again. And they went home, only now the donkey trotted with the tree upon his back and the old lady skipped along beside.

The tree fitted the cottage snugly as if it had sprouted there. The top touched the rafters, and the tips of the branches brushed the window on one side and the doorframe on the other. The old woman nodded her head and said, 'Time to make Christmas.'

Then Tante made cookies. She made gingerbread boys and girls. She baked almond cookies, cut into crescents like new moons, and cinnamon cookies, shaped like stars. When she'd sprinkled them with sugar and hung them on the

tree, they looked as if they'd fallen straight
from the frosty sky. Next she rubbed apples
until they gleamed like glass and hung these
up too. Tante put a red ribbon on a bone
for the dog and tied up a sprig of catnip for
the cat. She stuck bites of cheese into pine
cones for the mice and bundled bits of oats
to tuck among the branches for the donkey
and the cow and the goat. She strung nuts for
the squirrels, wove garlands of seeds for the
birds, and cracked corn into a basket for the
chickens. There was something for everyone
on Tante's tree, except, of course, for the
spiders, for they'd been brushed away.

When she was done, the old woman
nodded her head and said, 'Time to share
Christmas.'

Tante invited all the children in the village
to come and see the tree, as she did every year.

'Tante!' the children cried. 'That's the
most wonderful tree in the world!'

When the children had nibbled the

apples and sampled the cookies, they went
home to their beds to wait for Christkindel.
Christkindel was the spirit who went from
house to house on Christmas Eve and slipped
presents into the toes of their shoes.

Then the old woman invited the animals
to come and share Christmas.

The dog and the cat and the canary
and the chickens and some small shy wild
creatures crowded into the cottage. The
donkey and the cow and the goat peered
in the window and steamed the pane with
their warm breath. To each and every visitor,
Tante gave a gift.

But no one could give Tante what she
wanted. All of her life the little old woman
had heard stories about marvellous happenings
on Christmas Eve. Cocks would crow at
midnight. Bees could hum a carol. Animals
might speak aloud. More than anything else,
Tante wanted some Christmas magic that was
not of her own making. So the old woman

sat down in her rocking chair and said, 'Now it's time to wait for Christmas.'

She nodded and nodded and nodded her head.

Tante was tired from the cleaning and the chopping and the cooking, and she fell fast asleep. If the rooster crowed when the clock struck twelve, Tante wasn't listening. She didn't hear if the donkey whispered in the cow's ear, or see if the dog danced jigs with the cat. The old woman snored in her chair just as always.

She never heard the rusty, squeaky voices calling at her door, 'Let us in!'

Someone else heard.

Christkindel was passing the cottage on his way to take the toys to the village children. He listened. He looked and saw hundreds of spiders sitting on Tante's doorstep.

'We've never had a Christmas,' said the biggest spider. 'We were swept away. Please, Christkindel, may we peek at Tante's tree?'

So Christkindel opened the cottage door a crack, just wide enough to let a little starlight in. For what harm could come from looking?

And he let the spiders in as well.

Huge spiders, tiny spiders, smooth spiders, hairy spiders, spotted spiders, striped spiders, brown and black and yellow spiders, and the palest kind of see-through spiders came . . .

. . . creeping, crawling, sneaking softly . . .

. . . scurrying, hurrying, quickly, lightly . . .

. . . zigging, zagging, weaving, and wobbling into the old woman's cottage.

The curious spiders crept closer and closer to the tree. One, two, three skittered up the trunk. All the other spiders followed the leaders.

They ran from branch to branch, in

and out, back and forth, up and down the tree. Wherever the spiders went, they left a trail behind. Threads looped from limb to limb, and webs were woven everywhere.

Now the spiders weren't curious any longer. They'd seen Christmas. They'd felt Christmas, every twig on the tree, so they scuttled away.

When Christkindel came back to latch the door he found Tante's tree tangled with sticky, stringy spider webs. He knew how hard the old woman had worked to clean her cottage. He understood how dismayed she'd be on Christmas morning. But he didn't blame the busy spiders. Instead he changed their cobwebs into a gift for Tante.

Christkindel touched the spokes of each web with his finger. The twisted strands turned shiny gold; the dangling threads sparkled silver. Now the old woman's Christmas tree was truly the most wonderful in the world.

The rooster woke Tante in the morning.

'What's this?' cried Tante. She rubbed her eyes and blinked at the glittering tree. 'Something marvellous has happened!'

Tante was puzzled, as well as pleased. So she climbed on her stool, the better to see how such magic was spun. At the tiptop of the tree, one teeny, tiny spider, unnoticed by Christkindel, was finishing its web.

'Now I know why this Christmas is not like any other,' said Tante.

The old woman knew, too, that such miracles come but once. So, each Christmastime thereafter, she did not clean so carefully, but left a few webs in the rafters, so that the spiders might share Christmas. And every year, after she'd hung the cookies and the apples and the garlands on her tree, the little old woman would nod her head and say, 'Time for Christmas magic.'

Then Tante would weave tinsel among the branches, until the tree sparkled with strings of gold and silver. Just as her tree did on the Cobweb Christmas.

Just as Christmas trees do today.

# Starry, Starry Night

## Philip Ardagh

**U**p on a hillside, two strangers meet, one
sitting in the shadow of a great outcrop of
rock, the other heading up a dusty path on
foot.

'Lovely evening,' says the walking man.
He's young and bleary-eyed.

'Beautiful, isn't it?' says the other, from the
shadows.

'I wasn't expecting a full moon.'

'It isn't.'

'It isn't what?'

'A full moon.'

'Then why's it almost as bright as day?' asks the young man.

The other points up into the sky, the tip of his finger emerging from the shadows, and looking golden as it's bathed in starlight. 'The star!' he says.

'WOW! That's incredible! It's even brighter than before.'

'Don't tell me you didn't notice? It's a bit big and shiny to miss.'

'I've been asleep.'

'Asleep?'

The young man nods. 'Asleep, with strange dreams of wonderful music.'

'Wonderful music?'

'That's what I said.'

'You dreamt of music?'

The young man frowns. 'I suppose I did. I don't normally dream of sounds.' The truth

be told, he's been feeling very strange – very out of the ordinary – all evening.

'And what did this wonderful music sound like?'

'A chorus of angels.' He doesn't know where this thought – this sudden realization – came from, but that was *exactly* what it had sounded like.

'Do you often hear angels?'

'Of course not.'

'Then I was wondering how you knew what they sounded like.'

'Are you teasing me?' asks the young man. 'I'm confused . . . It was a dream.'

'Of a chorus of angels?'

'Exactly that.' The man punctuates his words with a nod of the head.

'Extraordinary!'

'That's what I thought.'

'What does a chorus of angels sound like?'

'Nothing on Earth.'

'That makes sense, I suppose. After all,

they are from Heaven.'

'It all seemed so *real*. It was so beautiful.'

'Like a great company of the heavenly host, singing the praises of God?'

'Er – yes, I suppose,' says the man, slipping his bag off his back and resting it on the ground.

'But you didn't actually see them?'

'No. Just heard them.'

'Maybe if you'd opened your eyes—?'

'It was just a dream, remember.'

'Of course. Silly of me.'

The young man looks around him, at the rock-strewn fields spreading up the hillside, bathed in the bright new star's heavenly light. 'Are these your sheep?'

'I'm looking after them, yes.'

'But there are hundreds of them!'

'The shepherds had to go somewhere in a hurry. I'm simply watching their flocks for them while they're away.'

'Isn't it a bit much to expect one man

to watch over so many?'

'There was one born this very day who will watch over a far greater flock.'

The young man furrows his brow. 'You don't sound like a shepherd.'

'This isn't my usual job.'

'You're just helping out?'

'Exactly.'

The young man rummages in the bag at his feet. 'I have some bread with me. Would you like to share some?'

'That's very kind. Thank you. I have nothing of my own.'

'Didn't the shepherds leave you anything to eat?'

'They all left in a hurry. They had other things on their minds.'

The young traveller takes a loaf of bread from the bag and tears it in two, giving the stranger the larger piece.

'Thank you.' The other takes it and eats. 'What's your name?' he asks.

'My friends call me Abas,' says the young man. 'What about you?'

'You can call me friend.'

'Thanks, Friend. There's no finer name.'

The other smiles in the shadows. 'A wise head on young shoulders,' he says. 'Where are you heading at this time of night?'

'Following the star . . . I've been travelling

for days. I knew I was tired, but I'm amazed that I dropped off to sleep like that.'

'There are strange forces at work tonight, Abas. This day is like no other that's gone before, or will come after.'

Abas listens to the words the stranger speaks, as much to their sound as to their meaning. 'There's something strange about your voice—'

'I'm sorry. Was I talking with my mouth full?'

'No, it's not that,' says Abas.

'This bread is delicious, by the way.'

'Thank you.'

'No, thank *you*. It is most generous of you to share your meal.'

'Do you know what?'

'What, Abas?'

'In a strange way, your voice reminds me of the music – the singing – in my dream.'

'There's a perfectly logical explanation for that.'

209

'There is?'

The stranger nods. 'There is.'

'What's that?'

'While you were sleeping, you heard me singing, and my voice came into your dreams and influenced them.'

'You sang like a host of heavenly angels?'

'I played my part.'

'Hmmm.' Abas is puzzled. 'What do you do when you're not watching sheep?'

'Whatever my master bids.'

Abas reaches into his bag and brings out his water bottle, made from skins. 'You'll be telling me that they didn't leave you any water, next.'

'I think the shepherds thought I had no need of it.'

'But all men need water!'

'I can't argue with that, Abas,' comes the quiet reply.

'Where have these shepherds of yours gone, Friend?'

210

'To see a baby.'

'A baby?' Abas can't believe it. 'They've left their sheep to go and see a *baby*?'

'Some people like babies.'

'That's not the point.'

'He's a very special baby.'

'Aren't all babies?'

The stranger smiles a brilliant smile. 'I can't argue with that. I've said it before, you're very wise for such a young man.'

'I'm not that young,' protests Abas, who's of the opinion that he's older than he looks.

'Young enough to live to see a time of great wonders and great change.'

'I'd just be happy to see the end of the Roman occupation.'

'After tonight, you'll see much more than that.'

'You know, Friend,' says Abas, 'I'm really glad to have met you.'

'You too, Abas,' says the other and, so saying, steps out of the shadows of the

outcrop of rock
and unfurls a pair
of golden wings,
'because I bring
you tidings of
great joy . . .'

## THE END OF THE BEGINNING

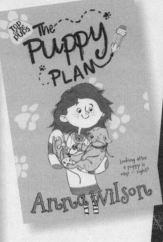

*Also available*

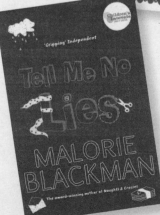